The Filthy Classics
A modern, erotic adaptation of Jane Austen

By Virginia Wade

This is a work of fiction. Names, characters, places, and incidents either are the product of the author's imagination or are used fictitiously, and any resemblance to any persons, living or dead, business establishments, events, or locales is entirely coincidental.

THE FILTHY CLASSICS, a modern, erotic adaptation of Jane Austen

All rights reserved.

Published by I Love Stacy
Copyright © 2011, 2012 by Virginia Wade
Cover art by Shutterstock/Conrado
ISBN: 1481212168
ISBN-13: 978-1481212168

Email: virginia@virginia-wade-erotica.com

This book is protected under the copyright laws of the United States of America. Any reproductions or other unauthorized use of the material or artwork herein is prohibited without the express written permission of the author.

First Edition: December 2012

Dedicated to Larry

Also available in paperback

Cum For Bigfoot, Volume One
Cum For Bigfoot, Volume Two
Jane's Playmates
Sarah's Playmates
The Filthy Classics Collection

Coming soon to paperback

Siren Island
The Stacy Series, Volume One
The Stacy Series, Volume Two

Follow Virginia at
http://virginia-wade-erotica.com

Contents

Pride and Penetration   1
Sense and Sexuality   51
Naughty Emma   95

Pride and Penetration

Chapter One

My sister, Jane and I, were helping my mother, Mrs. Bennet unload groceries from the back of her car when an enormous moving truck drove down the street. It was headed for the most expensive house in Netherfield Ranch.

My mother's eyes beamed with interest. "The new owners are moving in. I'll have to find out who they are." She was an unrepentant busybody who had to know everything about everyone in the area.

I rolled my eyes at my sister. "Here we go."

"She'll never quit trying to marry us off, Beth. You know that."

Jane, sweet, gorgeous, and blonde, never lacked for boyfriends. While I, on the other hand, was dark haired, fiery, and opinionated, the total opposite of a man magnet. They were scared shitless of me, and had always been, the spineless little weasels.

Our house was a sprawling two-story abode near the golf course, but, since daddy lost his job last year, we were in the process of foreclosure. Mom worked for a local Box Mart, I waitressed, Jane attended community college, and my younger sisters were still in High School.

Speaking of my younger sisters, Mary was the smartest in the family, and she preferred studying and playing World Of Warcraft to dating, while Cathy and Lydia preferred dating to studying. These airheads, as I referred to them, were frequently in trouble for either smoking at school, failing classes, or getting caught having sex with their boyfriends.

Aside from my father, Jane was the only person in the family I could relate to. She was hard working and smart. We shared the same dry sense of humor and general cynical attitude about love and life, having been rung through the dating mill and tossed out repeatedly. I personally was fed up with men. A bad break up last year had left me with a sour disposition, from which I had yet to recover.

Two days later, having completely forgotten about the new arrival to our little community, my mother announced at the dinner table, "He's single!"

Jane and I exchanged a glance, not knowing what the heck she was talking about. This happened often.

"Mr. Bingley! His name is Mr. Bingley. I heard from Greta Peterson, who was told by Holly Dexter, who overheard a conversation at the pharmacy, that the new owner of the white mansion is single." Her eyes shone with excitement. "Ladies! You have to wear something skimpy and parade around outside. Go walk the dog or something. Get his attention, for Christ's sake." She glanced at me. "Beth, you have the tits for this. Wear a tank top." She pointed at Jane. "And, you! Short skirts for you. Show him those mile high legs. Shake that pretty ass of yours. One of you has to snag him. Anyone who can buy a three million dollar house is certainly good enough for one of my girls."

Lydia looked indignant. "What about me, mom? Am I not good enough for Mr. Bingley?"

She demurred, "Of course, honey. You should try to get his attention as well. He might like them young."

Mary snorted. "Ugh. That's disgusting. He's probably old and bald."

"No!" snapped my mother. "Not at all. Susan Hicks and Loretta Bishop saw him at the country club yesterday. He's young and good-looking. He drives a Porsche!" She clapped her hands. "I love Porsches."

I stared at Jane. She looked amused, yet uninterested.

Daddy slapped the table, making the salt and peppershakers rattle. "It's settled then. Your mother has solved all of our problems. While this Bingley person is marrying one of our daughters, can you get him to write a check for the mortgage?" He held up his fingers, showing a space between them. "We're this close to being thrown out on our ass."

My mother pursed her lips. "Oh, stop it. The banks are overloaded with foreclosures. They won't even bother with us for years." She gave Jane a huge smile. "You and Beth should go for a walk and flaunt those hot young bodies. This neighborhood has an eligible bachelor. Go work the pavement." She shooed us away with her hands. "Now go! Snag a rich husband, and put your family out of misery."

Having been given our orders, my sister and I took the family Shih Tzu for a spin around the block, where the dog stopped repeatedly to lift his leg and urinate against each and every stationary object.

I wore a pair of shorts and a bland t-shirt. I kicked a pebble and grumbled, "This is ridiculous."

Jane watched in horror as Muffy squatted on an immaculate lawn. "I'm not picking that up."

There were strict rules regarding the removal of pet waste at Netherfield Ranch. I pulled on the leash, dragging the dog away in mid-shit, lest anyone perceive that the Bennet sisters had yet again befouled the neighborhood. The poor dog was forced to defecate in the street.

Whilst we were making a hasty and disgraceful exit, a golf cart approached in the distance, occupied by two men, who looked to be in their late twenties. As they neared, I cast Jane a look.

"Would that be *the* Mr. Bingley?" The tone in my voice was teasing. "OMG, Jane! We're about to encounter the *rich* bachelor."

She laughed, and, as always, her face lit up like a Christmas tree filled with angel ornaments. As the cart approached, the driver stared at Jane. She had yet to gain the upper hand over her amusement, and she giggled helplessly. He stopped the cart abruptly, forcing his passenger to hold on to the seat.

"Whoa there, cowboy. Are you trying to kill us?" The passenger wore a pair of sunglasses, but the chiseled curves of his face gave away the fact that he was incredibly handsome.

"Hello, ladies," said the driver, flashing a bright smile. His sandy colored hair matched the stripes on his shirt.

Jane grinned. "Hi."

"I'm new to the neighborhood." He held out his hand. "Mr. Bingley, at your service."

Reaching out, Jane shook his hand. "I'm Jane."

"This is my friend, Mr. Darcy." He turned to the dark haired passenger, who nodded, but said nothing.

"Nice day for a walk, isn't it?"

"This is my sister, Beth."

"Hello, Beth."

"Hi."

The way Mr. Darcy eyed me had my skin tingling, which was weird. He stared at my chest, or at least that's where I thought his eyes were. He had yet to remove the sunglasses.

"I'm having a house warming party Saturday night. You and your family are more than welcome to attend," said Mr. Bingley.

Oh, my God. My mother would just love that.

"That sounds nice," said Jane.

He eyed her with interest. "This neighborhood sure got a lot hotter all of a sudden."

Jane blushed. I rolled my eyes. *Give me a break.* These two wolves were on the prowl for fresh meat. I'd encountered the type before. Pulling on Muffy's lead, I said, "Thanks for the invite. We'll think about it."

Mr. Darcy removed his sunglasses and stared at me. I wasn't prepared for how handsome he was, and the shock must have been evident on my face. His eyes traveled up and down the length of my body, making my nipples harden instantly. This reaction was singularly peculiar, and, as my pussy throbbed, I wondered what the hell was going on? One look had done that? *Oh, wow.*

Saturday evening, as we prepared to go to Mr. Bingley's house warming party, I watched Jane curl her hair in front of the mirror that sat on her desk. Her room was decorated with frilly curtains and plush stuffed animals. Mine was plain like a dormitory at a military academy.

"He's cute, Beth."

I shrugged. "Yeah, I guess."

"I thought you were over Jeremy? Why are you still hung up on that loser?"

"I'm not."

"Then what's wrong?"

"Nothing."

"Aren't you even going to try to look nice?"

"Why bother?"

She set the curling iron down and stared at me. "For God's sake. Go put something sexy on, and quit moping. Would it kill you to have fun tonight?"

I bit my plump lower lip. "Fine." I got up from the bed and patted her on the shoulder. "You look nice."

"Thanks."

An hour later, at the Bingley residence, I took a glass of champagne and surveyed the surrounds. An investment banker, who had lived high on the hog until the economy tanked, had built the mansion several years ago. When the stock market crashed, so did his portfolio. The house had been empty for three years.

I recognized many faces of friends and neighbors. My sisters, Lydia and Cathy, giggled and joked, while Mary loitered by the appetizers, not being able to decide which one she wanted to eat. Mother was in conversation with Caroline Bingley, who was Mr. Bingley's sister. She seemed like a stuck up prig, and, from her posture, it looked as if she could barely tolerate my mother. Jane had Mr. Bingley's undivided attention, as they chatted by the dining room table.

"Looks like you made it."

I turned to find Mr. Darcy hovering over me. I had no idea he was so tall. "Uh...yeah." I mentally kicked myself for sounding like a complete moron.

"Your mother sure likes to talk."

I glanced at her. She had trapped several people, who were forced to listen to her senseless prattling. I nodded, not trusting myself to open my mouth and say something stupid.

"It's a nice night. You want to take a walk?"

I assessed him carefully, noting the pleasing gleam in his eye, the curve of his face, and the way his dark hair shone under the lights. "Okay."

In the backyard, we strolled towards the shorn lawn of the golf course. The sun had gone down, and the stars twinkled overhead.

I was the first to speak. "Do you live here too?"

"No. I have a place in town."

"Oh."

"What do you do, Beth?"

"I…waitress."

"I see."

I had been going to school, but my family could not afford two of us in college, so I had dropped out. They struggled now to pay for Jane's classes.

"Besides waitressing, do you have any other aspirations?"

This question irritated me. "According to my mother, I'm supposed to find a rich husband to save the family." I glared at him. "Are you rich?"

He looked stunned. "Um…maybe."

"Fabulous. Why don't you drop to one knee and propose, moneybags. Put us out of our misery."

Chapter Two

He smiled. "I've never encountered this approach before. My hats off to you for your…inventiveness."

I snorted. "Never mind. Well, I tried." I headed back to the mansion.

"Where are you going?"

He was hot on my heels. "To get a drink. My work is done here." His hand wound around my upper arm, halting my escape. He drew me to him. I struggled. "Get your paws off me!"

"Hold on just a second."

Did he have to smell so nice? And, boy, was he strong. Was he wearing a metal vest under that shirt?

"Don't you have any manners at all?"

I gasped. "You're the one all over me like a rash! Don't *you* have any manners?"

"I've never met anybody so irritating before. Stop struggling, you little minx."

His lips were suddenly on my neck, and I sucked in a sharp breath, completely floored. Pushing against him, I tried to get this hunk of man flesh off me, but it was nearly impossible. His hands were around my back, pressing me to the hard length of him. I could feel his arousal against my stomach, inflaming me instantly, which, in turn, horrified me. What an arrogant son of a bitch to think he could manhandle me in such a way! *Ugh. Men were pigs!*

As he covered my mouth, I groaned in reluctant acquiescence, and I just knew I would give in to this handsome lout. I thought of all the reasons why I shouldn't let a stranger grope me and tossed them out. The hell with it! I hadn't been kissed in months. My neglected pussy throbbed with lust; the wetness of my arousal dripped, dampening my panties.

"Oh, God, you're so sexy."

He pulled me into a darkened corner of the garden, and we dropped to the grass. His hands were suddenly everywhere, inching up under my dress to my thigh. I flung my head back and let him have me, not caring that he was a complete stranger and that I was behaving like a slut. I could hear laughter and music from the mansion; all the while, Mr. Darcy's finger stroked my pussy, eliciting a lengthy moan.

"Oh, ooohh…"

I grasped at his shirt, trying to undo the buttons. He worked to release his belt and lowered his pants. My dress was suddenly over my head, exposing a silky pink bra, which barely contained my abundant cleavage. He eyed me, touching the milky tops of my globes.

"You should take this off," he murmured.

I undid the clasp and let the material fall. My breasts were in his hands to overflowing. He took a nipple into his mouth and suckled, which shot a flame of heat into my pussy. I reached for the formidable looking erection between his legs and tugged on it.

"Oh, Jesus. You're a hot one."

I pushed against him until he was on his back. "Let's see if you have something I'm interested in."

His brows rose in aroused amusement. "I think I do."

"You're pretty full of yourself, aren't you?"

"Never had any complaints before."

"Maybe they were drunk."

He looked slightly offended. "Aw, come on."

I wrapped my hand around his cock. "Well, so far, so good."

"You're killing me."

I closed my lips around him and sucked, producing a manly groan from him. His hands went to the top of my head, as I worked him with skill and ease. I enjoyed sucking cock, and this one was magnificent. It was so long it butted up against the back of my throat. Suppressing the gag reflex, I bore down on him until my lips touched his hairy mound.

"Oh, Jesus."

I licked the sides of the shaft and balls, taking the soft sacs into my mouth and prodding them with my tongue.

"Aaahh...Beth..."

He dripped with my saliva. Not wanting to squander another second, I pulled down my panties, straddled him, and lowered onto the waiting cock, driving it in deep.

"Oh, ooohh..."

I hadn't had sex in so long, that I felt a twinge of discomfort from his size, throbbing and pulsing inside of me. As I adjusted to him, I began to move, thrusting back and forth. I dug my fingers into the firmness of his chest and rode him for my own pleasure. My breasts jiggled with the movement of my hips, and he grasped them, tweaking the nipples.

Not remembering the last time I had had an orgasm, I felt the edges of one hurtling towards me with each thrust. The swiftness of the approaching storm had me moaning helplessly, quivering on top of a man I didn't know at all. That hard cock was my only concern, and it pleased me having it inside my pussy, working its magic.

"Oh, God!" I shuddered on top of him, gasping and groaning, as release savaged my body and left me trembling with tiny aftershocks.

"You look so good on me."

I collapsed on top of him. "Um…"

He chuckled, "I feel a little used."

"I'm good now. You can go."

He laughed, his chest rumbling. "You're not going to leave me like this, are you?"

That wasn't a half bad idea. "I…might."

"You're a tease, Ms. Bennet."

The hardness of him was still firmly lodged. I could feel it throbbing. I slid from him and enclosed it with my fingers. "I suppose you want me to suck this?"

"That…would be nice."

"I guess I could. This once."

"You're a sweetheart."

Taking him into my mouth, I worked vigorously, sucking and drawing on the hardened end. His hands went to the top of my head, where he held me gently while I pleasured him. I smelled myself on his hot flesh, which was arousing, spurring me onward to take him in deeper.

"Oh, that's so nice."

Gagging, I swallowed him whole. He groaned and pulled out of my grasp, manipulating himself with skill. I waited for him to squirt, holding my mouth open.

"Oh, God!"

The end burst with a torrent of white, hot fluid, which I caught on my tongue. Several more streams followed, and I ingested every bit of what he offered. Then I set about licking him clean.

"You…are so good." He sat up and grabbed me, pulling me to him. "We should date."

"I'm not looking for a relationship right now."

"Let's just fuck then."

"We already did."

He chuckled, "You're not gonna just use me and leave me, are you?"

I reached for my dress. "I have to get back." He watched me pull up my underwear.

"What's your number?"

"Why?"

"So I can call you. Take you out."

I tossed the dress over my head. "Give me your phone. I'll plug it in."

"I left it in my jacket in the house."

"I'll meet you inside then." I slipped into my shoes and walked away.

"Hey! You can't just leave me like this."

"Yes I can."

I found Jane with Mr. Bingley talking in a corner, oblivious to the world around them. My parents were glued to poor Ms. Bingley, who looked like she could use a stiff drink. Lydia flirted with someone who seemed far too old for her, while Mary and Cathy played video games in the den with several friends.

There was a bathroom near the kitchen, and I went in to make myself presentable. I stared at my reflection, removing mascara that had smudged beneath my eyes. The smile on my face could hardly be contained, as I grinned, feeling relaxed and happy. I'd had the best sex in months with a hot guy who would perhaps date me. I could smell his cologne on my body, and it teased my nose, reminding me of the sensual delights we had shared under the stars in the backyard.

Leaving the bathroom, I went to find Jane. I walked up to her near the buffet table. "Hey you."

She turned. "Where have you been?"

"Um...I might've gotten to know Mr. Darcy better."

Her mouth dropped open. "You're kidding?"

I shook my head. "Nope."

"You little slut."

"He was…really nice."

"I can't believe you."

"I couldn't help myself. I haven't been with a guy in like forever." Lydia and Cathy ran by, laughing. "Let's take a tour."

We strolled down a hallway tiled with light brown travertine.

"I really like Mr. Bingley," said Jane. "He's a computer designer. He's part owner of the company. I found out that Mr. Darcy's filthy rich. He has like tons of real estate, and his family owns a hotel."

"Great for him."

We were near an open door, which was a book-lined study. Mr. Darcy and Mr. Bingley stood together, conspiratorially. Bingley was laughing.

"That's the best piece of ass I've had in a long time," said Mr. Darcy, chuckling.

I gasped.

He turned and stared at me. *What a pig!* Pivoting on my heel, I stalked down the hallway.

Chapter Three

Jane and Mr. Bingley were now officially dating, which pleased my mother to no end. I never gave Mr. Darcy my phone number, and he could fall off a cliff for all I cared. He'd lived up to my rather low expectation of men by bragging to his best friend about our garden rendezvous. Whenever I thought of him, I steamed with anger, fanning the resentment I had for the opposite sex.

To make matters worse, my distant cousin, Mr. Collins, had arrived for a visit. He was an annoying, nosy, and perverted man, who looked at porn on the computer openly, no matter who might be in the room. Jane and I went to great lengths to avoid being alone with him, but my mother continued to push us together in the hopes that I would date him or worse, marry him. Yuck!

At dinner, the high, nasal quality of his voice grated on my nerves.

"You have to visit me," said Mr. Collins. "You'd love Gracefield College. The dean, Mrs. Catherine de Bourgh, was kind enough to rent me a little house on the property. It's a fixer upper, but I love it."

"That sounds nice," said my mother politely.

Lydia and Cathy exchanged a bored glance.

"Dean de Bourgh has been like a mother to me. When I first started teaching, I was a mess. I couldn't even get the class schedules right. I got lost three times on the first day. She escorted me around personally." He shook his head, his baldness gleaming under the dusty chandelier. "What a wonderful woman."

"Sounds like it," murmured Jane. She pushed her peas with the tip of her fork.

"Oh, she is. Her house is amazing. It's huge." He

held out his arms. "Like a mansion. It's in a little enclave called Rosings Manner. You should all come visit. I can give you a tour."

I glanced at Jane and she hid a smile.

"Fascinating," I said.

"Now, girls," admonished my mother. "The mountains are beautiful this time of year. Maybe we should take a little trip."

I grabbed my plate. "Gosh, I'm full. I'll just clean this up." Jane was right behind me.

We left the room as our cousin was saying, "Your daughters are gorgeous, Mrs. Bennet. Jane especially."

"Why thank you, Mr. Collins."

I turned to Jane in the kitchen. "Ugh. When's he leaving?"

"Not soon enough."

The next day, I was on my feet for hours, taking orders in a neighborhood restaurant I had worked in for more than a year now. I knew most of the customers by name. My boss, Craig, was a sweetheart. He was the only reason I had stayed in this crappy job for as long as I had.

Lydia and Cathy came in. I worried for a moment that they had ditched school, but it was after three. They had been forced to attend summer classes due to poor grades. They brought a friend with them.

I breezed over. "Hi, guys."

"Hey," said Lydia. "I want a…hmm…? I'll have the cherry pie."

"That's healthy." I eyed the guy with them, admiring how cute he was. He looked far too old for my teen sisters.

Lydia noticed my attention. "Oh, this is Mr. Wickham. He's a friend."

What was he doing hanging out with my dippy

sisters? "I'm sorry, but who are you?"

He grinned. "Ah, the protective vibe. I get it. I work at the game store down the street. They caught me on my break."

"Okay."

"I want a burger, Beth," said Cathy. "Fully loaded."

"What would you like, Mr. Wickham?"

"A burger sounds great." His smile was blinding.

"Drinks?"

"Yeah, I'll have a diet Coke," said Lydia.

"Me too," added Cathy.

Mr. Wickham said, "Make mine a regular."

"Sure. Be right back."

After my sisters and the friendly Mr. Wickham had been served, they left, but not before the dashing Casanova slipped me his number on a napkin. I pocketed the item and mulled over calling him for the rest of the day. Seeing that I had been single for an embarrassingly long time, I threw caution to the wind and texted him. He was thrilled to hear from me and asked me out. We found ourselves at the movie theater that night.

"What are you doing with my little sisters?"

"Just hanging. Nothin' wrong with that, is there?"

"No, but Lydia's a total airhead."

He shrugged. "She's cute." A gleam shone in his eye. "But, I have to admit, older women are hot."

I tingled pleasurably. He was referring to me; at least I hoped he was. "Thanks."

"Lydia says you have new neighbors who are filthy rich. I might've heard of them before."

"Yeah?"

"I know Mr. Bingley a little. His friend, Darcy is…well, I've worked for him in the past."

This was a surprise. "Really?"

"His family owns hotels and stuff. I managed one for a while. They accused me of some shit I didn't do and fired me."

"That sucks."

"Yeah, it was bad. I had to live in a shelter for a while."

My mouth hung open. "That's terrible."

"That family thinks they own the planet." He took a sip of his drink. "You know how rich people are. They treat their employees like shit. Crap wages, crap benefits, the works. Worst job I ever had." He added, "Worst people I ever met."

This only confirmed what I already thought of Mr. Darcy. "Well, you seem to be doing all right now."

He grinned. "I am. Got an apartment. I'm on my feet." His grin was sheepish. "Ah…I like a little on-line gambling, but…I've cut back."

"That can be addictive."

"No shit," he muttered.

We went to an outdoor mall after the show and wandered around. I genuinely enjoyed his company, and when it was time to go home, he kissed me passionately in his beaten up Geo Metro. I waved to him as he drove away, hoping I would see him again.

I got the shock of my life after entering the house. My best friend, Charlotte, was in the living room chatting up Mr. Collins. They looked like they'd known each other for years.

"Hey, Charlotte. What are you doing here?"

"I came over to see you, but you were out." She stood and hugged me. "You didn't tell me you had such a friendly cousin."

Whether I hid the horror on my face or not, I wasn't sure. "Uh, yeah. This is a family…member."

"Charlotte and I have a lot in common, Beth," said Mr. Collins. "She loves Steampunk almost as much as I do." He beamed from ear to ear. "And, cats. She has two!"

"Is that so?"

"Well, I do love cats." Color had risen on her cheeks.

I pulled Charlotte to the side. "What are you doing? That guy is a moron."

Her expression hardened. "No he isn't. Just because you attract the losers, doesn't mean they're all like that."

Ouch. That hurt.

"We're going out tomorrow." She threw back her shoulders and smiled tightly, defiantly. "There's a Steampunk convention."

"I...I'm sorry. I didn't mean to sound like a bitch. You guys should go to the convention. I'm actually happy you like him. He does have a job. That's sayin' something." I wasn't going to mention his online porn proclivities. She could find that out on her own.

"Thanks for the vote of approval." Charlotte still looked a little ruffled around the edges.

"I'm beat. You guys should hang. I'll talk to you tomorrow, okay?"

"Sounds good, cousin Beth."

"Good night."

They sat on the sofa and resumed their conversation.

As I lay in bed that night, I thought about Mr. Wickham. He was tall, thin, and adorable. The oddest thing happened, though. Mr. Darcy's face continued to creep into my thoughts. This occurred during the day as well. I'd be taking an order at work and there he'd be in front of me, until I blinked and the customer came into focus. My temporary insanity was freaking me out.

Getting out of bed, I woke my computer and typed his name into a search engine. Several pages worth of information popped up on his family, hotels, and businesses. His photo had been taken at a charity dinner, and he stood there surrounded by thin models with vacuous smiles. I closed the laptop, disgusted.

Ugh!

Chapter Four

My sister, Jane begged me to go to Mr. Bingley's for a party I did not want to attend.

"Go without me. I'd be the third wheel anyway. You guys should have privacy."

"Please, please, Beth. You gotta come."

I groaned, "Why?"

"Cause it's Saturday night and you don't have a date."

"I'm catching up on TV."

"That's stupid. Get dressed and come with me. Don't leave me all alone with mom and Lydia. Please."

I rolled my eyes. "Fine. I guess I can go for an hour."

Jane jumped up and down excitedly. "Yay!"

Throwing on a short, dark purple dress, I ran a brush through my thick, brown hair and felt a pang of self-satisfaction at the way the long tresses shone. I took care of myself by watching what I ate and going to the gym, but it had always been my hair that had gotten the attention, that and my full breasts.

Daddy refused to go, so us girls took off laughing and chatting towards the big white mansion at the end of the lane. All the lights were on, and shiny cars were parked down the street.

"Oh! Girls! Look at those Mercedes. Look at that Lexus!" Mom's eyes were huge. "There are rich men here tonight. Your orders are to snag one of 'em. Put your father and I out of our misery."

"Mom, for Christ's sakes. It's the new millennium, not the turn of the freaking century," I griped. "Women don't need men to rescue them anymore." I glanced at

Jane's shining face. She beamed with happiness. "Jane's got a guy."

"There isn't a ring on her finger yet. We need absolute confirmation first, before we can start to celebrate."

Good grief. If only daddy could get a job.

Lydia and Cathy ran up ahead and disappeared through the front door. They would more than likely play video games all night. Mr. Bingley had a basement dedicated to pinball machines, an old-fashioned video game parlor, air hockey, pool, and darts.

Jane linked her arm through mine. "You'll have fun, Beth. We can hang with Bingley."

I begrudgingly admitted, "He's a nice guy. You're lucky."

"Thanks."

I wasn't in the house five minutes, when I perceived Mr. Darcy standing with Bingley's sister, Caroline. They had their heads together laughing. I glared at him from across the room until his lips rose in a smirk, which should have made him look like the pompous ass he was, but it had the opposite effect. Did he have to be so darn good looking? He obviously took excellent care of himself, because his physique was lean and toned. He dressed impeccably in a pair of pressed jeans and an elegant designer shirt. He was more than likely wearing daddy's salary from last year, if you included the sparkling wristwatch.

I took a glass of wine and stewed in my resentment, which suited me just fine. While mom chatted and laughed and Jane flirted with Mr. Bingley, I entertained myself by watching people and waiting until the hour was up, so I could make my escape.

"It's good to see you, Beth." The object of my irritation had come up behind me.

"I'm leaving in a minute."

"So soon?"

"Uh-huh."

"Oh, dear God!" My mother spilled a glass of red wine on the white carpet. "Oh, I'm so sorry."

"That's all right. I'll have someone get that," said Caroline Bingley crisply.

"You're not still mad about that...other night, are you?" Mr. Darcy's warm breath was on my neck.

"The fact that you have a big mouth and have to brag about your exploits?"

"Aw, come on. Bingley's my best friend. We were just...well...you shouldn't have heard that." He looked contrite.

"It really doesn't matter. You're not my type."

"You seemed to like me all right on the grass."

I refused to look at him. "I was drunk."

He laughed, and it sounded rich and smooth. "I don't think so. Let's take a walk."

I tingled everywhere. "Forget it."

"I'm not talking about another stroll through the garden, unless that's where you wanna go."

"In your dreams."

His hand wrapped around my upper arm. "Let's get some air."

As we passed my mother, I overheard her asking, "So, how much money do you make a year, Mr. Crawford?"

I sucked in a shocked breath. *God! How embarrassing!* Mr. Darcy had heard that as well. He shook his head amused. If I thought escaping my inappropriate family would be as easy as leaving the house, I was wrong. Out by the pool, Cathy and Lydia swam naked, while a group of men watched. I nearly died of mortification.

"Lydia! Cathy! What are you doing?"

"We're swimming, silly. Get in."

My hands had gone to my hips. "I can't believe this. There are a ton of guys watching." I glowered at the lecherous hounds and gave them the evil eye. "Go away. Go watch porn or something."

Mr. Darcy held two towels. "Here, girls. Use these when you get out." He glanced at me, light sparkling in his eyes. "Nice night? Isn't it?"

I turned on my heel and headed for the house. I hadn't gotten far, when I was redirected into the study by my nemesis, who wouldn't go away.

"Stop manhandling me."

"Give me your phone number."

"No."

He closed the door. The room was lined with mahogany bookcases, and a heavy looking desk occupied the center. He pulled me to him.

"All I can think about is that night in the garden." His lips grazed my neck. "You're the hottest piece of ass I've had in a long time. I wouldn't mind another."

I pushed against him. "That's romantic. Does that line actually work?"

He seemed confused. "When I fucked you the last time, I didn't have to say two words to you."

My mouth hung open. "What a pig!" I turned to leave, but he grabbed me.

"I can be anything you want me to be, Beth."

His arms were around my waist, and I felt the bulge of his erection pressing against my back.

"You've got some nerve, if you think I'm sleeping with you again."

"Who said anything about sleep?"

He dragged me to a chair, where I found myself

draped over his knees. I fought to dislodge myself. "Get off! Stop, you bastard. What the hell are you doing?" His hand came down on my bottom, and I gasped. *He just spanked me!* This arrogant son of a bitch spanked me. Before the shock of what he had done had truly penetrated my brain, another slap came. *That hurt!* "Ouch! Stop it!"

"I think a good spanking is exactly what you need, Ms. Bennet."

To my horror, he lifted my dress, exposing my thong, which left nothing to the imagination. I squirmed and thrashed trying to get off his lap, but his strong hands held me virtually immobile, as yet another slap sounded. Whack. My bare bum stung.

"You're a pervert, Mr. Darcy!"

"And I've never been happier about it."

"I just bet."

His hand massaged my buttocks, stroking and provoking. I didn't want to enjoy him touching me, because he was a bastard, but tingles began to erupt in my tummy, signifying that my body was a traitorous bitch. *Damn!*

"I'm getting off." I slid from his lap and sat on the floor, glaring at him.

"Now that's an idea."

Did he have to look at me like that? "I'm sure you can find any number of ladies who'd be willing to *get you off* tonight."

"I'm looking at her right now."

I scoffed, "Ugh, dream on." I stood, but I didn't get far. I found myself in his arms, being held far too close to his steely length. Did he have to smell so good?

His lips descended, and I meant to tell him no. I was just about to…but…the kiss sucked out whatever brain matter I had left in my head. My response was to rest my palms against his shirt and open my mouth for his silky tongue. Manly hands cupped my bottom, pulling me to his hardness.

"Oh…"

The next thing I knew, I was attacking him with my hands and mouth. The mortification I felt was quickly replaced with a blazing lust that had smoldered and now burst into something scorching and wild.

"God, you're amazing, Beth."

"You're a bastard."

He chuckled and bit gently into my neck. "I'll be your bastard any time you want, honey."

"I'm not your honey." I grasped his cock, which was encased in his jeans, and undid the buttons, letting the organ spring free. "This is the only thing I want from you."

"You wound me."

Lifting my dress, I pulled down my thong and leaned against the deck. "Fuck me, Mr. Darcy. Get that cock over here."

His brows lifted. "You sure are full of demands."

I thought he would object, that smug bastard, but he was behind me in a flash, his hot hands on my heated flesh.

"Oh, my God." Just knowing he was there, that his hands were on me, sent me off the cliff. What was it about him that made me want him so badly? He wasn't even my type. We had nothing in common, except for sex.

"Are you ready for me, Ms. Bennet?"

I groaned, "Yes."

"You sure?"

"Stop playing, and fuck me!"

He chuckled, and, with one fluid thrust, he was buried deep. The feeling of fullness was incredible. His cock was magnificent in length and function, or was it the man himself? As it slid in and out of my dripping hole, I clung to the desk, knocking over pencil holders and piles of letters.

"This is so good," he groaned.

"Don't stop."

His hands were on my hips, his cock plunging deep, and I was out of my mind with lust. Each thrust brought me closer to the ultimate goal of release. Never had a cock felt this good before. He'd turned me into a total slut, and I wanted even more. The sound of skin smacking against skin filled the room along with our moans. The revelers were outside the door drinking and laughing, while I was having hot, nasty sex against a desk.

"Oh, Beth!"

"Don't cum yet."

"Arrggg…"

"Just…one second more." I let my face drop to the desk, nicking the side of my eye on the edge of a small picture frame. The pain diminished as the first inklings of climax exploded in my belly. "Oh! God! Oh-oh-oh…"

"Yes! Cum on my cock, you Bennet bitch." He thrust forcefully, embedding to the hilt and gasped. "Ooohh…aggg…"

I collapsed on the desk spent, breathing raggedly. When I was at last able to speak, I said, "This won't happen again."

"We'll just see about that."

Chapter Five

Not long after the party at Mr. Bingley's house, Jane came to me crying. "He's gone."

"What?"

"Mr. Bingley's gone. He has to work in California for a couple of months. He left this morning."

My mouth dropped open. "You're kidding?"

Tears were in her eyes. "No. I thought he liked me. I thought we would…well, never mind."

"What an asshole. How could he just leave like that?"

She shrugged. "I don't know."

I had gotten a black eye from having sex on top of the desk. It was a constant reminder of what a slut I had been, which angered me even more. I was sure Mr. Darcy had told Mr. Bingley of our little interlude, because braggarts can't keep their mouths shut.

"Look, if he can't see how wonderful you are, he's a moron. Who does that?" I shook my head. "Oh, hell, they all do. That's the game. Lead us on, screw us for a while, and then goodbye. It's typical."

Her eyes watered. "He was different. I know he's not a moron. He'll be back."

I harrumphed, "Don't waste another second thinking about him."

"He's the only one I want." She sniffed delicately.

I groaned. "There are other guys. We'll hit the town tonight and get drunk. Let's not mope in the house, okay?"

"Maybe."

One week later, I got a phone call from Charlotte, and she had big news. She married Mr. Collins over the weekend in a small civil ceremony. I nearly fell off the chair; I was so shocked. She'd invited me to her house, and, since I had nothing planned for the weekend, I packed a small bag and headed for the mountains. Plugging the directions into my GPS, I found their house on the edge of the university property, near Rosings Manner.

Charlotte ran out to greet me. "You found us!"

"Yeah, it wasn't hard."

"I'm so glad to see a familiar face."

"I posted on your page on Facebook this morning."

She grinned. "I know, but seeing people in person is better."

"How are you?"

"Great. I love it here. I'm so happy to be married." She held out her left hand. Her engagement ring sparkled.

"That's nice."

"Thanks. My new husband is amazing."

We went into the house, and I got the tour, which didn't take long. Their furniture was eclectic, the cats were numerous, and Mr. Collins' idea of artwork consisted of movie posters from the 1950's and Charlotte's framed cross-stitch designs. My friend seemed perfectly happy in her marriage and her new house. Being the cynic that I was, I had to let go of my judgment and agree with her for once.

I soon found out that we had been invited to Dean Catherine de Bourgh's for dinner. Mr. Collins went on and on about what a wonderful, thoughtful woman she was and how she'd been mentoring him. By the time we arrived at her sprawling mountain home, I was developing a headache.

The house was huge with enormous windows that showcased panoramic views of the valley below.

"This cost two million dollars," said my eager cousin.

"Wow. It pays to run a college, I guess."

"She comes from money."

"Oh."

Dean de Bourgh was a matronly woman, with sharp eyes and a dry tongue. "Welcome to Rosings Manor, Ms. Bennet. How do you like our mountain?"

"It's beautiful, Mrs. de Bourgh."

"Thank you." She eyed me. "You're a waitress?"

Why did that sound like an insult? "Um, yes."

"How, wonderful." Her tone suggested otherwise.

We were in a cavernous living room with an enormous fireplace. A door closed, and two men entered, one of whom I recognized and loathed on sight! Mr. Darcy. What the hell was he doing here? He smiled at me smugly, and I looked for something to throw at him. An expensive sculpture on an end table would do nicely, but they would probably sue me to get their money back.

"Beth. It's so good to see you again."

"Ugh…hi."

His friend laughed, "Not your greatest fan, is she? I bet there's a story there."

"This is Dr. Fitzwilliam, Beth."

"Hi." I shook his hand. He had a friendly face with smile lines etched into tanned skin. "What kind of doctor are you?"

He grinned. "The best kind."

Mr. Darcy supplied, "Internal medicine."

"Good. He can sew you back up after I stick you with something."

"I guess you're still sore about that spanking, huh? I see the eye is better."

God, that was embarrassing! His friend had heard that. "I'm not talking to you."

I sat near Charlotte and ignored him, but it was nearly impossible. His presence was a total distraction, and, throughout dinner, all I could do was try not to stare at him. The reason he was here was that Dean de Bourgh was his aunt. Dr. Fitzwilliam was a family friend. After dinner, I excused myself and wandered around the dimly lit house, staring out the huge windows into the valley below, which was dotted with lights.

"We can't seem to escape each other, can we?"

I turned to find my nemesis behind me. "I guess."

"You still haven't given me your phone number."

"Ain't gonna happen either."

He chuckled, "We should date."

"No. That's the worst idea yet."

"How come?"

"Don't you have a couple of super models stashed somewhere? Rich guys like you are supposed to love brainless bimbos."

"You like to insult me. That's fine. Actually, I kinda like it." He drew me into his arms. "I kinda like you."

"No!"

He kissed me anyway, and I melted instantly. I would beat myself up about it later, but right now, I just wanted his hands on me. I kissed him like a starving person who'd been abandoned in the desert. He was my oasis, even if he was far too handsome and far too rich. We collapsed on a nearby sofa and began to strip the clothing off our backs, one glorious piece at a time. Naked, I attacked him and rubbed my pussy against his thigh, moaning.

"You're a wild woman." He sounded hoarse.

"She sure is," said a third voice, which startled us. It was Dr. Fitzwilliam.

"Oh, MY GOD!" I grabbed my clothes and held them to me.

"Hey, I'm a doctor. I've seen breasts before."

Mr. Darcy chuckled, "You're still sneaking up on people. Nothing ever changes."

"I heard moaning. I went to investigate. It's like my civic duty."

Why wasn't he leaving? I stared at him in horror.

"She sure is pretty." His interested gaze was on my thighs. The front of his pants had begun to bulge. Was he totally turned on by us or was it by me? I glanced at Mr. Darcy. The state of his friend's pants had not escaped him. He looked a little sheepish.

"We've shared girls in the past. It's…a practice left over from our college days."

My tummy tingled at the thought. Did I want to have sex with two really hot guys at the same time? Two sets of hands rubbing and pleasing me. Two sets of mouths…oooh! This had possibilities. "What are you suggesting?"

He shrugged. "We could have fun, Beth. You might like it."

Fitzwilliam knelt before me, touching my thigh. "Darcy always gets the gorgeous, smart ones. It's not fair."

His touch had ignited a yearning in my pussy, which throbbed distractedly. "Um…I…guess we could mess around."

The attractive doctor smiled and kissed my thigh, which made me gasp. He massaged my leg gently, yet with growing persistence. While he was thus engaged, Mr. Darcy kissed me, fondling my breasts and tweaking my nipples to stiff perfection.

"Oh…"

I had two gorgeous men pleasuring me, and it was heaven. My thighs were being separated, and a wet tongue had found its way to my shaved mound, where it drove into the folds of my pussy and began to spear me repeatedly.

"Um...dirty boys..."

My hands drifted to Fitzwilliam's scalp, holding him in place, while he serviced me intimately. The feel of him in my pussy sent my heart racing, while my body throbbed with pleasure. I grasped Darcy's cock and massaged him, while he continued to kiss me.

"Oh, God, Beth."

An idea formed, and I pushed gently at the doctor, detaching him from my love hole. Sliding from the sofa, I leaned over and took Darcy's cock into my mouth, sucking him noisily. From behind, I felt hands on my bottom, stroking and massaging. Then the tip of a fat cock prodded me, lubricating itself in my wetness.

"Ohhh...yes," I gasped. "Do that."

"I will."

He ran his tool up and down my slit and then plunged deep, filling me to the brim. While I sucked and slurped, an incredibly horny man pounded me from behind.

"Beth. That's so nice."

Mr. Darcy's cock was in my throat, making me gag noisily. A rush of saliva cascaded down the veined length, pooling at the base. With every suck, I felt a sensual tug in my female anatomy, which left me tingling. My pussy walls clamped around the cock and pulsed.

"Oh! Shit. I'm getting close."

The doctor slid out suddenly. I turned to grasp him, while holding Mr. Darcy's cock. I sucked him fiercely, eliciting a lengthy groan.

"It's almost here...oohh..."

I watched as he pumped himself, glistening wet with my saliva. The end looked like a pink spongy mushroom and deliciously fat.

"I'm..."

I held my mouth open waiting for him to squirt. A

second later, a stream of hot milk burst free, speckling my lips and tongue. I sucked him then, eating his spunk and cleaning him with each pass of my tongue, until every last drop had been wiped away.

"She's amazing," he murmured.

"She is."

I returned to Darcy's cock and gagged on his length. Fingers were in my pussy, driving in deep. The doctor rubbed something fabulous inside of me that had me gasping. *Oh, my God. What is that?* It must have been some sort of hidden erogenous zone, because I could feel the edges of an orgasm forming with alarming swiftness.

"Cum on my cock, Beth. I can feel you want to."

"Oh! Jesus. Don't stop!"

"The g-spot always gets 'em."

I devoured the cock whole, until I gagged. My make up had more than likely been wiped off, but I could have cared less. I'd never had sex with two men before, and I was seeing the advantages of such an exercise. My entire body buzzed with the need for release, and as I began to convulse, Mr. Darcy shot his load deep into my mouth, both of us moaning in unison, experiencing our bliss at the same time.

Chapter Six

After I had made myself presentable, I went to find Mr. Darcy. I encountered the doctor instead. He was in the broad hallway before the living room.

"I...guess I should thank you for...uh...you know."

I was so embarrassed. "It's okay. I don't usually have sex with strangers, but..." Why did that sound like a lie? I'd slept with Mr. Darcy shortly after I met him. *God, I'm turning into such a slut.* "Uh, never mind."

"He's mentioned you before and your family. I can see why he's attracted to you. You're absolutely gorgeous. If it doesn't work out, I'd be more than happy to step in." He grinned.

"That's sweet of you, but we're not exactly dating." *And, that makes you an even bigger slut. Shut up!*

"He said you weren't that fond of him, but he's not such a bad guy, Beth. I've known him forever. I can count on him for anything. He's given me and Bingley some great advice over the years."

"Sure."

"No, really. The reason I'm a doctor is because of him. My mate, Bingley's still single and not shackled to this chick he was gonna propose to. He's saved us more than once from making some boneheaded decisions."

My mouth fell open. "What chick?"

"I don't know. Somebody he met this summer."

Anger practically had steam coming out of my ears. "Excuse me." I found Mr. Darcy pouring himself a glass of wine. Everyone had gathered around Dean de Bourgh as she held court on the sofa. "I have to talk to you."

"Yeah. What is it?"

I pulled him into the hallway. "Is it true that Bingley was going to ask Jane to marry him?"

He pursed his lips. "Where did you hear that?"

"It doesn't matter. Is it true?"

"I really don't know."

"I think you do. I think you had something to do with him going away."

He looked uncomfortable, which confirmed what the doctor had said. "She's in love with him, asshole!"

He scratched his chin. "Don't get all bent outta shape, Beth. I just...I thought...well, she didn't seem head over heels. I thought I was doing him a favor. I—"

"You self-righteous bastard! She loves him. It broke her heart when he left." I had to find my handbag and get the hell out of here. "You shouldn't meddle in other people's lives. What are you, some kind of control freak? Some friend you are!"

"Look, I was trying to save him from making a mistake."

"Like you saved Wickham? Firing him and throwing him out on his ass."

He looked shocked. "What?"

"I've heard all about it. He had to go live in a homeless shelter after you were done with him."

His eyes blazed with anger. "Now, wait a minute. He worked for us, yes, but the reason he was fired was that he stole fifty thousand dollars from payroll! He has a gambling addiction. I could've forgiven that, but when he tried to molest my sister, Gorgy, that was it. He's lucky I didn't report him to the police. He's lucky I didn't beat his fucking ass."

This was new information, but it didn't change anything. "I'm going. You...have a nice life."

"Wait! Don't leave, Beth. This is ridiculous. Let's

talk about it."

"You've already talked enough. Goodbye, Mr. Darcy."

It took more than two weeks to get over my anger. I would never forgive him for ruining Jane's happiness, but what he'd said about Wickham remained with me. If he was a thief and a molester, then perhaps it was wise to stay away from him, charming as he might be. I threw myself into work and finalizing the plans for a mini vacation with my aunt and uncle. Every year we went to explore a new part of the state, and this year was no exception. They wanted to stay at The Grand Hotel near Pemberley Farms, which was a scenic property near the national forest. I loved old hotels, and I looked forward to having a break from work.

As I dragged my bag downstairs, I encountered daddy. He had come in from mowing the lawn.

"You're going already?"

"Yes."

"You'll have a nice time, honey."

"I will, daddy."

"You and Jane are my pride and joy."

I hugged him. "Oh, that's sweet."

He sighed. "I just wish I had some control over Lydia. She was out all night."

"What?"

"She came home early this morning, but God only knows where's she's been."

"You have to start laying down the law with her. Don't let her walk all over you. It's bad enough she's flunking all her classes." That moron couldn't even pass the summer classes. Ugh.

"We're doing the best we can, honey."

The doorbell rang. That was my aunt and uncle. I hugged him. "You should ground her ass. She needs to know there are consequences for bad behavior." Having five children in quick succession had worn my parents out, and, by the time Lydia and Cathy had been born, they were at the end of their ropes. "Gotta go, daddy."

"Have a good time, Beth."

"I will."

My aunt and uncle Gardiner were a happily childless couple who enjoyed taking me on little trips. We got along famously, and, as we drove to Pemberley Farms, I was able to catch up on all the exciting things that had happened to them over the last year. These included renovating their house, a trip to England, and a new boat, which they kept on their lake.

I sat in the backseat and stared out the window. "How was England?"

"It was amazing." Aunt Gardiner turned to me and smiled. "We'll have to take you some time."

"That would be wild."

"We were in London, but I want to see the countryside next time."

"I'd love to go to Paris too."

Uncle Gardiner chuckled, "That's our plan as well."

"Great minds think alike."

"The Grand Hotel at Pemberley Farms was built in 1922," said my aunt. "It's supposed to be haunted."

"I love creepy places."

"The grounds are beautiful. We booked two rooms. There's a silver mine tour, a lake, and hot springs. We can do as much or as little as we like."

I settled into the seat. "Sounds perfect."

Two hours later, we pulled into a tree-lined drive that led to an enormous structure, which was set amidst a mountain and surrounded by trees. The gray stone hotel, with its sweeping rooflines and gothic, mullioned windows, looked formidable, yet intriguing. We drove to the entrance, where a bellboy came out and got our things. Once we'd unpacked and freshened up, we headed outside and toured the grounds.

By midday, we ate lunch on the terrace, and I excused myself to use the bathroom. As I rounded a corner, I literally bumped into Mr. Darcy, of all people.

I stared at him in shock. "What are *you* doing here?"

He looked far too happy to see me. "I own this hotel."

Why was that not a surprise? "Great. Excuse me."

"Won't you talk to me?"

"No." I brushed past him, but he held my arm.

"Don't leave, Beth." He drew me to him. "How have you been?"

I pushed against him. "I...none of your business." I didn't care if I was being rude.

"Are you here for the day?"

"Something like that."

"I'm having dinner with my sister. Please join us."

"Can't. I'm here with people."

"Bring them. I don't care."

I pulled my arm free. "Look, it's nice of you to offer and all but—"

"No, buts. Just come to dinner."

I stared into his sexy eyes, cursing myself for tingling everywhere. Why did I always react like this when he was near? "I'll think about it."

"She'd love to meet you. I'd love to spend time with you." His expression was earnest and pleading and far more intense than I ever remembered.

I was weakening. "I'll ask my aunt and uncle."

When I returned to the table, they were ready to explore the sights. We were going to the lake.

"We've been invited to dinner," I announced.

"Oh?" My aunt smiled. "By whom?"

"The owner of the hotel." A shocked hush met this declaration.

Later that evening, after I'd tried on all of the outfits I had brought and settled on the lesser of the evils, we headed to the private section of the hotel, where I introduced my aunt and uncle to Mr. Darcy. He wore dress slacks and a pressed white shirt. His cologne, with spice and sandalwood undertones, teased my nose and sent my sensual radar into high gear.

"Your hotel is lovely, Mr. Darcy," said Aunt Gardiner.

"Thanks. You guys are welcome to stay as long as you like. It's on me. I can lend you a car as well, if you want to drive to the mountains. Or I could take you myself."

His gaze drifted to me, and my tummy fluttered.

My aunt and uncle exchanged a glance. Uncle Gardiner spoke, "That's incredibly generous of you."

"Not a problem." He smiled gregariously. "Here she is. Here's my sister, Gorgy."

A pretty teen breezed into the room, wearing jeans and a sparkly yellow top. "Hey!"

Mr. Darcy stood and hugged her. "Glad to see you're finally off the computer."

"I love NeoPets. I can't help it."

"Meet some wonderful people, Gorgy. This is the lovely Ms. Bennett and her aunt and uncle Gardiner."

"It's nice to meet you." She smiled at me. "I've heard about you."

Uh-huh. What did *that* mean? I sat and placed the napkin in my lap. "That's a pretty top."

She beamed. "Thanks."

"Now tell us, Mr. Darcy," asked my uncle. "What

places do you recommend for sightseeing around here?"

His face split into a pleasing grin. "Lots. I'd be happy to take you myself." He winked at me.

Chapter Seven

"Hey! Wait up." Mr. Darcy strode towards me in the hallway before my room.

"You were so quiet at dinner."

I shrugged. "I guess. Your sister is sweet."

"She likes you."

Did he have to stand so close? "Um, it's been a long day."

His hands cupped my face. "Beth."

"No, don't." He was about to kiss me, and my protest sounded flimsy. "Oh, no."

"Oh, yes."

His lips met mine, igniting the fire that had been smoldering in my belly. Why did he always affect me this way? I wanted to push him away, but instead, I wound my arms around his neck and pressed myself to him.

"We can't do this."

"Let's go in. I want you so bad."

"No."

"Give me the room card."

I kissed his neck. "Hum…"

He took it out of my hand and swiped it, opening the door. We stumbled into the room and began to undress. Hands were suddenly everywhere, caressing, undoing the hooks at the back of my bra and stroking my heated skin.

"You're so not my type."

He chuckled, "I doubt that. I think I'm exactly what you need."

We fell to the bed, where I rolled on top of him and stared into his attractive face. "You can have any woman you want. Why me?"

This question had surprised him. "You're the biggest pain in the ass I've ever met, that's why. I like my girlfriends to abuse me, clearly."

I giggled, "You're a bit of a masochist, huh?"

He slapped my ass. "I give as good as I get."

His cock was beneath me, hard and thrusting. I grabbed it. "Maybe I should bite this?"

Passion flared in his eyes. "You should." I took him into my mouth, and he groaned. "Oh, Beth."

Working the engorged tip, I sucked him aggressively, until my lips began to feel puffy and my jaw ached. He held up his balls, which smelled deliciously musky, and I sucked each into my mouth in turn.

"I've something I'd like to eat." He pushed me to the bed gently.

"Oh, yeah?"

"Yeah."

He buried himself in my snatch, lapping up the juices of my arousal and prodding my clit with the tip of his tongue.

"Oh, yes."

"You never disappoint me, Beth."

"Shut up and suck."

He laughed at that, and continued to drive his soft tongue into my hole, until I arched my back and thrust my pelvis into his face. My hands were on top of his head, pressing him into me, enjoying being attended to in this naughty manner. When I could feel the wistful edges of bliss drawing near, I pushed him away.

"Come here." I held out my arms.

"I've another idea."

He pulled me off the bed, standing behind me with his hands on my hips. With one thrust, he was buried deep.

I gasped, "Oh, God, yes!"

"I knew you'd like this, you dirty girl."

"I am. Ooohh...fuck me."

He slid in and out, drilling me over and over. I grasped the bedspread and held on for dear life, while he worked me unrelentingly. The fervor of his need signaled the rather hasty arrival of my orgasm, which had me stifling a scream. I convulsed against the bed, contracting my vaginal muscles and arching my back. I couldn't remember an orgasm ever being this intense before. That had happened too fast, dammit! He continued to hammer me, and, to my utter astonishment, I felt the possibility of another developing rapidly.

"Oh, God! Mr. Darcy!" There was no way this was happening. I'd never been multi-orgasmic before. That was something they made up in books. It wasn't real or was it? "Oh, my...shit! Fuck me, *hard!*"

He plunged into my dripping pussy, filling me completely while I moaned with ecstasy. My entire body shuddered with the second climax, and I struggled to breathe, as sensation after sensation bombarded me.

"That was hot." He pulled himself free. "You should turn around."

I felt incredibly relaxed. All my muscles had turned to mush. I smiled lopsidedly. "Wow."

"No kidding."

Taking his wet cock into my hands, I sucked him vigorously, wanting to please him just as he'd pleased me. He smelled like my pussy, which turned me on even more. The tip expelled clear fluid, and I licked it away.

He groaned, "That's so nice."

I laved to his balls and suckled the sacs individually. Then I crammed them both into my mouth.

"Oh, God, Beth. I'm close."

He massaged his cock before my face, until the tip

burst open and spurted my tongue with salty goodness. I ate every last bit of the cream and licked my lips.

We collapsed on the bed and lay in his arms, snuggling into his warmth.

"Are you ever going to give me your number?"

"Yeah."

"Thank God. We should definitely date."

"Is that such a good idea?"

He laughed, "We've slept together how many times now? I'd like to have a relationship with you. I don't want to fight anymore." He was thoughtful. "I mean, I love the fighting too, but, I want you in my life. I want to see you every day."

I rose over him. "Really?"

"Yes, really."

"But I don't look like a super model."

He growled, "I don't give a shit! I don't want a super model." His hands tightened around me. "I want you, Elizabeth Bennett."

"I might be able to accommodate yo—" My cell vibrated on the nightstand and I reached over to grab it. "I might be able to do that."

"That'd be nice," he said dryly.

"Hello?"

"Beth!"

"Mom?"

"Your sister Lydia's been kidnapped. The police are here right now. I think she's with that Wickham person."

I sat up. "What?"

"They were seen being thrown into a van on Main Street. Witnesses got the license plate number. They're trying to find them right now. Oh, my God! I'm out of my mind with worry."

I glanced at Mr. Darcy. "Lydia's been kidnapped

with Wickham. The police are at the house."

"I'm sorry to spoil your vacation, Beth, but I thought you'd want to know."

"Thanks, mom. I'm coming home."

"Oh, honey, I'm so sorry," she sobbed. "I hope my baby's okay. I hope they didn't kill her, those bad men."

"I'll call you back in a little bit." I snapped the phone shut. "Shit."

Mr. Darcy looked sober. "He's always in trouble with somebody."

I slid off the bed and reached for my clothes.

"What are you doing?"

"I have to go home."

"Right now?"

"Yes, right now! My family's in crisis. My stupid sister is probably being murdered as we speak."

He watched me dress, looking thoughtful. "What about you and me?"

"Um, I don't know. I have to go take care of this right now. We'll see."

My answer bothered him. He looked angry, but he was fighting it. He took my phone and opened it up. "I am not letting you go again without getting your number." He scribbled it on a complimentary hotel notepad. "We aren't over, Beth. You hear me?"

I stepped into my shoes. "Yeah, I hear you." I hated to be so cool and abrupt, but my family needed me. They were probably freaking out right now with worry and fear. "I…you should call me sometime."

His expression remained impassive. "I will."

We were in the car within fifteen minutes heading home, under a pall of unhappiness. My little sister had ruined my vacation, and now I worried that she had lost her life in the process.

Chapter Eight

We got the call four days later, telling us that Lydia had been found safe and sound. My mother had been on the verge of a nervous breakdown, climbing the walls with worry. Loan sharks had kidnapped Mr. Wickham. He owed a great deal of money to shady people. Apparently, my aunt and uncle had negotiated for Lydia's release, which had astonished me. How they even knew who these horrible people were was a mystery.

As Lydia burst through the front door in a flurry of overly dramatic gestures, I rolled my eyes at Jane, who shared my feelings on this issue. We both new Lydia was a twit and that whatever misfortune came her way was well earned. This did not give her the right to stress out my mother.

"Lydia!" Mom embraced her. "My poor, Lydia! You had us so worried."

"I'm fine, mom. They got the jerks who kidnapped us! It was so awesome. It was like *Mission Impossible*. They busted down the door with guns. Those bums didn't even put up a fight." She seemed almost high with giddiness. "They were gonna smash Wickham's kneecaps to get him to cough up the dough he owed 'em. What a loser. I dumped him, by the way." She plopped down on the sofa. "Then Mr. Darcy came in and took care of everything."

"What?" Now *this* had my attention.

"Oh, shit! I wasn't supposed to say that." She held her hand to her mouth. "Never mind."

I glanced at Jane. Her eyes sparked with interest.

"Darling, none of that matters," cooed my mother. "You're home now safe where you belong."

Cathy and Mary flanked her on the sofa.

"Tell us about the kidnappers? What did they look like? Did they hurt you any?" asked Cathy.

Lydia snorted. "No. They tied us up, was all. They were boring."

I pulled Jane aside. "So, Mr. Darcy had something to do with this."

"Sounds like it."

"I never told you, but Wickham used to work for him. He was fired for stealing money. He also tried to molest Darcy's younger sister."

"Really?"

I nodded. "Yeah. I wonder how much it cost to pay off the loan sharks?"

"Probably a lot."

Her look was earnest. "You really like him, don't you?"

I sighed. "Yes."

"He's a nice guy for what he did. He found Lydia and took care of everything."

"What about you? What about Bingley?"

"I don't know. If he'd been interested in me, he wouldn't of left. I've gotten over it now."

I didn't believe her for a minute.

Jane and I went for a walk after dinner, enjoying the sunset and the last days of summer. I had Muffy on a lead, and, when he squatted in Mr. Holmes's immaculately tended front yard, I let him.

"Oh, men," complained Jane. "I'll never understand 'em."

"Me either."

"I'm tired of being led on and dumped. It sucks."

"You deserve way better than that, Jane. You're such a sweetheart."

She linked her arm with mine. "I can see our future

now. We'll be old ladies together with like ten cats and rotting cheese in the fridge."

I laughed, "Sounds about right."

A golf cart came in our direction, and damned if it wasn't Bingley himself in the driver's seat! My sister and I stopped in our tracks. He pulled up to us.

"Jane."

"Hi."

"Um, can I talk to you?"

"Are you back to stay, Mr. Bingley?" I asked.

He looked worried. "Hopefully. I really need to talk to you, Jane. Can you get in?"

"Sure." She whispered for my ears only, "I'll be back in a sec."

I watched as they drove away and wondered at his strange expression. The cart stopped at a distance, and I witnessed him get out, drop to one knee, and it seemed as if he'd produced a ring. Jane hugged him, and they kissed passionately as several neighbors drove by ogling.

"Well, jeez louise. How about that?" I stared in shock, wondering if my eyes had deceived me. I tugged on Muffy's lead. "Come on, little pisser. Let's go home."

Later that night, after the celebration of Jane's engagement to Mr. Bingley had died down, I settled in front of the TV to catch up on my *Ghost Hunter* shows. I was halfway through the second episode when my cell buzzed.

"Hello?"

"Yes, is this Elizabeth Bennett?" asked a stern sounding voice.

"Yes."

"This is Catherine de Bourgh. You'll remember me from the dinner you attended at my house."

"I remember. Hi. How are you?"

"I'm calling because I've heard that you're about to marry my nephew. Is this true?"

"Um, you mean Mr. Darcy?"

"Yes."

"I...don't think so. He hasn't asked me. We haven't even dated really."

"That's all fine and good, but I must know what the schedule is, because I'm leaving for Europe on the fifteenth. If the wedding's later, I won't be able to attend. He's my beloved sister's son after all, and I can't dishonor her memory by not being at her only son's wedding."

This flabbergasted me. "Um...I...will have to get back with you about that."

"You have my number now. I don't like to be left out of the loop on these things. I've some marvelous ideas for the reception, and I know the best caterers. Please call me as soon as you know when you're getting married."

I held the phone from my face and stared at it, as if it had turned into an alien object.

"Are you still there?"

"Yes. I'll let you know as soon as I know. Thanks...for calling."

"Very well. It was nice meeting you, Ms. Bennett. My nephew is a lucky man to have you, dear."

"Th-thank you."

I was so shocked by this conversation, that I stared at the wall for a good hour before going up to bed. The next morning, I dressed in shorts and a t-shirt and left the house to clear my mind. I headed for the golf course, and, as I rounded a corner, a golf cart appeared. Mr. Darcy was in the driver's seat. He was alone.

"Fancy seeing you here."

"What are you doing?"

"I came to find you."

"I know you helped Lydia. She told us."

"She's got the biggest friggin' mouth." He tried to appear angry, but his smile would not abate. "You look really good." Hungry eyes devoured my chest.

"So do you."

"How about you get in, little lady, and let me take you for a ride."

I laughed, "You sound like John Wayne."

"I have a proposition for you."

I stepped into the cart. "Oh, yeah?"

He nodded. "Yup. I think you should marry me, Beth."

"I got a phone call from your aunt. She wants to know when the wedding is, so she can plan accordingly."

"I heard about that. You didn't deny it outright, so I thought I might have a chance." His eyes glimmered. "Do I have a chance with you, Ms. Bennett, or are you gonna just fuck my brains out every time we meet?"

"Um…both sound really good," I laughed, feeling little tingles fluttering in my tummy.

"Is that a yes?"

I kissed him. Those full lips looked irresistible. With any luck, he would drive to Bingley's house, and we could get a head start on the honeymoon, because I was suddenly incredibly horny.

The End

Sense and Sexuality

Chapter One

My mother looked at me unhappily. "Well, that's it. We're out on our asses." She held up a piece of paper.

"What do you mean?"

"That bitch got a court order. We have until the fifteenth to pack up and get out."

We were in the large kitchen, surrounded by gorgeous granite countertops and expensive appliances. Since the divorce, my mother had refused to leave the home she had painstakingly remodeled. The break up had also left her angry and bitter. To compound matters, Daddy died a month ago in a car accident, and his new wife wanted us out with a passion.

"We knew this might happen." I hugged her. "It's gonna be okay, mom. We'll figure something out."

"The house belongs to her son, John, now. His wife, Fanny, is coming tomorrow. She's bringing her architect brother, Edward. They're renovating or something. They'll ruin everything I've worked so hard for." She began to cry.

"Mom. It'll be okay. We've been through worse. We're gonna survive this."

"What's wrong?"

My younger sister, Marianne breezed into the room. She was blonde, blue eyed and as pretty as a porcelain doll. I was the opposite, with dark hair, a slightly chubby body, and a perpetually stern expression, which had resulted in a crease between my eyes. A little Botox could take care of that, if I had the funds.

"Daddy's wife is making us leave."

Marianne sighed. "That's not a surprise. Does Meggy know?"

Our youngest sister was still in school. "Mom will tell her later."

"That sucks." She opened the refrigerator and retrieved a bottle of soda.

"We have house guests tomorrow," said mother miserably. "John's wife, Fanny, and her horrible brother will be here."

Marianne shrugged. "So?"

Anger clouded her features. "So somebody has to prepare the goddamned guest room. I'm not doing it."

"I'll do it. Let me take care of everything."

"I have to make some calls. I have to find us a place to live."

"Let me make those arrangements." She already had enough to worry about.

She held up a newspaper. "There's a three bedroom condo that might be worth looking at."

I glanced at the court order. "I can bring this to work and have one of the lawyers look it over. Maybe it's not even legit." I was a part-time legal secretary.

"I really don't care, Elinor," she said petulantly, glancing around, as tears filled her eyes. "Twenty years and I have to say goodbye. I love this house."

Poor mom. Things had gone badly for her these last two years. First her husband had an affair with his best friend's wife, resulting in a scandal, and then the divorce, which left her emotionally and financially ruined.

The next day, as I grabbed my keys and left work, I drove home wondering if Fanny and Edward had arrived yet. I met Fanny last Christmas and disliked her immediately, but Edward was a pleasant, quiet man who I found interesting. He had to be at least thirty and still single from what I remembered.

An extra car was in the driveway, so they had arrived. I wondered how my mother was holding up? Walking into the house, I found Marianne and Edward playing Wii in the living room, which was a surprise. Tall, with dark hair and blue eyes, Edward paused when he saw me, his expression filling with interest. I had the strangest reaction to him, as my tummy tingled with little butterflies.

"You should watch this, Elinor. I'm beating him pretty good."

He set his controller down. "I think I'll stop now before it gets any worse. Thanks for the game, Marianne."

Her mouth fell open. "Oh, come on. We're just getting started."

"I'm hardly a worthy opponent," he muttered, smiling. He got to his feet. "Hello, Elinor. How are you?"

"Great. How are you?"

"Just fine, thanks. I've been wanting to talk to you. Can we…go somewhere?"

"Sure." I walked by him. "The study is private."

"Sounds good."

My dad's office had been cleared of all his things. He'd removed the books and the computer. It was a hollowed out space now. I turned to Mr. Ferrars, wondering what he wanted to talk about.

"I'm sorry about throwing you out of your own house."

"It's not your fault."

"No, but…I feel responsible."

"You're not."

He sighed. "It's a crappy situation. What will you guys do?"

"Mom's looking at a condo." I had to clarify

something. "Look, it's okay. Mom was obnoxious about leaving. She made it her mission to make life hell for my dad after he took off with *that* woman. A lot was done out of spite."

"I can understand her anger."

That statement was mildly surprising coming from him. "She didn't want the divorce, but daddy did and now…he's gone."

He looked grave. "I'm sorry for your loss."

"Thanks."

"My sister and her husband want to live here. I'm supposed to help them make changes." He appeared less than thrilled. "I'd rather redesign a burger joint actually."

I laughed, "Well, good luck with that. We'll be outta here soon enough, and you guys can do whatever you want."

"You're taking this really well."

I shrugged. "What else am I gonna do? It is what it is."

"My sister wants an ultra modern look with clean lines and chrome."

I cringed. The house was cozy Country French with antique furniture and comfy sofas. "I'm glad I won't be here to see it."

"Well, there you are," said Fanny as she entered the room without knocking. "Edward has some wonderful ideas for the house, don't you?"

"Yes," he said simply.

Fanny was short, with curly hair and a thick waist. Her nose was round, and her cheeks were puffy, which gave her a piggish look.

"Hi, Fanny."

"Hello, Elinor. It's good to see you again."

"It's been so long." I had no idea what to say to this

creature I disliked with a passion. "You look…healthy."

"Thanks so much. I'm really sorry you have to move. I wish there was some way to avoid that, but I don't think it's possible."

"We're making other arrangements. Mom's taking care of it."

"Yes, she told me. You'll be renting a condo. How nice." The tone in her voice gave away her obvious distain for such an idea.

I forced a smile. "Smaller space is less cleaning." *What the hell else am I going to say to this twit?*

"Oh, that's for sure." She smiled, but her eyes remained dull.

Later that night, after everyone had gone to bed, I found myself with Edward in the living room with a movie on. We shared the sofa, and I stared at him covertly, admiring the way his cheekbones added to the sexiness of his profile. I'd been attracted to him from the first day we met. He'd always been a bit of a mystery. His family, who I had yet to meet, was well to do. They owned several businesses including the architectural firm he worked at. His brother, Robert, was also an architect. From what I gathered, their mother was an overbearing shrew who liked to meddle in her children's lives and dictate how they should live.

Edward asked, "So, who are you dating now?"

This question caught me completely off guard. "Um…no one right now. How about you?"

"I've been too busy with work."

"Oh."

His attention was still focused on me, and I felt a twinge of arousal and nervousness. I'd only had two lovers in my twenty-four years, and I found myself shy around men, although I loved sex. I had a collection of dildos that would make a prostitute blush. The phrase, dating my dildo, certainly referred to my miserable excuse of a love life.

"You...shouldn't be single, Elinor."

Was he making a pass at me? "I don't want to be. You shouldn't be single either." I caught a strange glimmer in his eye that I wondered about. It disappeared almost instantly.

He scratched the back of his neck. "I...maybe we could...um...never mind."

Now, *that* had my undivided attention. "Could what?" It was disappointing watching him withdraw into himself. He was almost painfully shy.

"It's nothing."

Feeling emboldened, and down right slutty, I placed my hand on his thigh. His sharp intake of breath told me that I had shocked him profoundly.

"Everyone's asleep," I whispered. "We're adults. Nobody would have to know if we...fooled around a little." I could not believe I had just propositioned someone in this manner. Goody, goody Elinor had just put out the red light. *Oh, boy.*

The look on his face was priceless and the bulge in his jeans telling. "I...I've always found you attractive."

That was the confirmation I needed, as I leaned in and kissed him. It took all of three seconds for him to grab me, haul me onto his lap, and devour my mouth like a seafaring sailor starved for female attention. Straddling him, I ground my pussy against the hardness of his cock and bit gently into his neck, producing a throaty groan from him.

"Oh, my God, Elinor."

His hands were under my shirt, molding my breasts. I wanted to feel him on my naked skin, and I flung the shirt over my head and unclasped the bra.

"Edward." I attached myself to his mouth and drove my tongue in to battle with his. "Take your pants off." I burned with need, not having had a lover in forever. My arousal was wetting my panties.

I slid from his lap so he could undo his jeans. He pushed the denim down his thighs. His cock escaped from the slit in his silk boxers, and I went to grab it.

"Good God!" he gasped.

My aggressiveness shocked him, but I didn't care. My only thought at that moment was to be pleasured by his tool, and, for that to be successful, I needed him nice and wet. Sucking him down my throat, I gagged until I had reached his mound. He smelled delectably musky and sweet, like baby lotion. When my saliva ran down the veined shaft, I shoved my pants down, underwear and all and climbed on top of him, lowering on his hot, wet tool. Feeling sluttier than I could ever remember, I fucked Edward in the living room of my mother's house, not caring in the least if we were seen.

"Oh, Jesus."

"Oh-oh-my-God!"

I ground down on him and used him for my pleasure. This was so much better than my dildos. His hands were on my hips guiding me back and forth, while my breasts jiggled invitingly in front of his face. He managed to get a nipple into his mouth, and he bit on it gently, which sent me galloping into oblivion, as the force of a shockingly strong orgasm threw my head back.

"Edward!"

"Yes. Take me. Do it."

Shuddering and gasping with tiny convulsions, I milked his cock for long moments, drawing out the pleasure as long as I could. Satiated and drained, I rested on his chest while he throbbed inside of me. I raised myself and let him pop out. Sliding from the sofa, I grabbed the object that had made me cum and shoved it down my throat.

"Oh, Elinor. God…yes."

He felt like a piece of wood, he was so hard. I took his balls into my mouth, smelling myself on him. His fingers worked his phallus and he massaged vigorously, while I sucked his soft sacs and prodded them with my tongue.

"That's so nice. I wonder…would you…would you like this?"

He wanted me to eat his jizz. "Yes." I held open my mouth, waiting for him to squirt.

"Oh, fuck, Elinor…I'm…going to…oooohhh…"

A spray of white cream suddenly had me closing my eyes. His cum splashed my mouth and dribbled out of the corners, dripping to my breasts. He sure seemed to have a healthy quantity of spunk. It was no small feat lapping up the excess fluid, but I gave it my all. It wasn't every day I had this opportunity, and Lord only knew when it would happen again.

Chapter Two

If I had thought sleeping with Edward would have been the beginning of a relationship, I was wrong. He took various photos of the house, made notes about the changes Fanny wanted, and left the next day. I fell into a funk for a week, wondering why he was so standoffish. When he hadn't bothered to call me, I went out on the town with Marianne and got rip-roaring drunk, flirting with every man that crossed my path.

Mother had signed the lease on a three-bedroom condo on the other side of town, and, with the help of some of my co-workers, we moved most of the furniture via U-Haul. We had so much stuff, mom had to rent a storage unit for what would not fit into the cramped condominium. After an exhaustive moving in process, we were finally seeing the end of the tunnel.

Our garbage disposal broke on the fifth day, and not being able to get hold of the landlord, our neighbor, Mr. Brandon, came over to help us. He was an Iraqi war veteran who now worked for the post office.

"I think maybe the reset button is out."

His head was under the sink. I had to empty it, and the countertop was crowded with cleaning supplies.

"Whatever you can do, Mr. Brandon, would be fantastic," said mom. She'd not showered yet, and her hair was a mess.

I stood nearby and loitered, admiring the way a small portion of his butt crack was visible above his jeans.

"Try to run the water, and see if it works."

I turned on the faucet and flipped the switch, which made the garbage disposal growl. "I think it works." I glanced at mom. "Well, that was easy."

She looked relieved. "Thank you so much, Mr. Brandon. You should stay for lunch."

He crawled out from under the sink, grinning. "I'd love to."

I set the dining room table, and we had left over chicken salad and salami sandwiches. Marianne breezed into the apartment with her keys in her hand, which were attached to pink, fuzzy balls.

"Oh. I didn't you know we had company."

Mr. Brandon's eyes widened at the sight of her.

"This is our neighbor, Marianne. He helped us with the garbage disposal.

She smiled politely. "Hi."

He held out his hand. "Nice to meet you."

Marianne shook it and sat. "What's for lunch?"

I glanced at the empty plate. "We had leftovers."

"That's okay. I ate at the mall." She worked for a department store. "I saw Meggy and her friends down by the pool."

Mother announced bluntly, "Mr. Brandon's a bachelor."

An awkward silence filled the room, and Marianne and I exchanged a look. I stood and took my plate. "Well, it was really nice of you to help us. Thanks so much."

His pleasing yet bland face lit up. "Whenever something breaks, ladies, please call me."

"We certainly will," said my mother.

"Lunch was delicious."

"Thank you."

After Mr. Brandon left, Marianne and I went to find the laundry facility in the building. Wearing flip-flops, she slipped on the cement stairs and fell hard, bouncing down the remainder to the next floor.

"Marianne!" I raced to her just as a man appeared.

He was tall, dark haired and shockingly good looking.

"Oh, God! My ankle's killing me." She held her foot in her hand, her eyes closed with pain.

"What happened?" asked the stranger.

"She tripped."

He bent down before Marianne. "Do you think something's broken?"

She met his gaze. "I...I'm not sure. It hurts."

"Can you stand?"

"I don't know." He got her to her feet. "Ouch!" She held up her left leg. "Oooh...crap."

"Let me help you." With effortless strength, he lifted her into his arms. "Where's your apartment?"

Marianne stared into his eyes. "Aren't I heavy?"

He grinned and shook his head. "We'll find the service elevator."

"We can't use that. We don't have access."

"I do."

"Oh."

A few minutes later, we were home with Marianne on the sofa and a cold compress on her ankle. Her chivalrous rescuer's name was Mr. Willoughby, and his family owned the condominium complex. He hovered obsequious and attentive.

"Well, you sure were helpful, Mr. Willoughby," said mother. "That's two handsome, helpful men in one day."

Marianne grinned. "He's way cuter than the other one."

Mr. Willoughby's brows lifted. "Is that so?"

She nodded.

He sat next to her on the sofa. "I'm partial to damsels in distress, especially when the damsel is totally hot."

"Or you're just worried we'll sue," I said cynically.

Mother gasped, "Elinor!"

"I'm joking."

"I think it's just a sprain," he said. "Give it an hour or so and then try to stand. You should be all right."

"Would you like something to drink, Mr. Willoughby?" asked my mother.

"A soda would be nice." He stared at Marianne. "I saw you move in the other day."

"Do you live here too?"

I sat in a chair and listened to their conversation.

"No, but I'm here often to oversee things."

"We used to live in a nice house, but my dad's family kicked us out."

"Marianne, do we need to rehash that right now?"

"Why not? It's true. Daddy married a horrible woman, and then he died in a car crash a month ago. Mom got totally screwed in the divorce."

"Marianne!" My mother looked horrified. "We don't need to discuss these things with everyone, honey." She handed him his drink.

"Thanks." Mr. Willoughby appeared amused. "I see lots of people who've fallen on hard times. The foreclosure crisis has done a lot of damage."

He seemed sincere, and his eyes were honest. I found myself liking him. My sister seemed enamored as she beamed brightly. Over the course of the next thirty minutes, they talked about everything from *The Hunger Games* to Adele. They both loved the television shows, *Big Brother* and *True Blood*, and Coldplay and Maroon 5 were favorites. Mother had gone into the kitchen to clean up, and I sat, feeling like I was intruding on a conversation between close friends.

After Mr. Willoughby left, Marianne announced, "I'm in love!"

"You only just met him."

"So what? I don't need to spend eight months with someone to know that he's the one for me." She looked exuberant; her eyes sparkled. "We're going out tomorrow night. I can't wait." Getting to her feet, she grimaced. "Ouch."

"Do you need help?"

"No. I got it." She hopped on one foot towards the bedroom. "I have to tweet everyone I know right now and tell them."

Mother stood in the doorway with a dishtowel in her hands, looking stern. "The poor man. He doesn't even know what hit him."

I laughed at that.

That was the beginning of the whirlwind courtship of Marianne and Mr. Willoughby. He picked her up the next night and took her out to dinner. After they came home, they were in the living room talking for hours. The next night, they went to an art festival and the evening after, to the movies. Mother invited our neighbor, Mr. Brandon, over to dinner, and all Marianne could talk about was Mr. Willoughby. Mr. Brandon wasn't a fan of Marianne's dashing suitor, but he did his best to appear polite and interested.

One night, as I made my way to the bathroom, I witnessed Marianne and Mr. Willoughby in a rather compromising position in the living room. He sat on the sofa and she on the floor with his cock in her mouth. I was so shocked I stood there for a good minute, until he groaned and the tip burst with semen, spraying Marianne in the face. I ducked into the bathroom and stood against the door with my chest heaving.

Chapter Three

Seeing Marianne servicing Mr. Willoughby had made me horribly horny. I went to my room and locked the door. From the drawer of my nightstand, I withdrew a pink, rubber dildo. I certainly could not count on a man to see to my needs, so I had to do it myself.

I took off my nightgown and got in bed, spreading my legs and tingling in anticipation. The dildo was the perfect size for me, not too big or too small. As I ran it up and down my moist slit, I sighed with contentment. I could play with myself for as long as I liked, and no one would bother me. Once the toy was slick with my arousal, I began to thrust it in. At first I would only dip it slightly. Then as the sensations spread and my chest flushed, I drove it in deeper.

"Oh, God…"

I pulled on it slightly, letting it move in and out, while my right hand manipulated my nub. I pleasured myself like this for long minutes, forming an image of Edward in my mind. The night we had spent together replayed itself over and over. As I began to convulse and shudder, I thought about how perfect his cock had been, and I wondered if I'd ever see it again. He'd been an amazing lover. I tossed my head to the side and clamped my teeth together, trembling with bliss.

"Ooohhh…Edward…"

I lay there for a while with the dildo buried deep. I pulled it out slowly and placed it on the nightstand. I would get up in a minute and wash it off, when I was sure Marianne had gone to bed. I'd heard the front door, and I knew Mr. Willoughby had left.

Over the next three weeks, my life became a

predictable pattern of work, shopping, cleaning, and helping mother with odds and ends. Marianne and Willoughby were going strong, and she was rarely home now. Mom and I watched our favorite TV shows and chatted about life in general, while Mr. Brandon joined us on occasion. He was becoming a good friend, and he listened attentively when I talked about Edward and my concerns about Marianne. I felt she was getting in far too deep and far too soon with Mr. Willoughby.

To illustrate this point, Marianne came home one night in tears. She ran to her bedroom and slammed the door and wouldn't come out for three hours! I eventually got her to open the door.

"What's wrong?"

She could barely speak; she was so upset. "He-he-broke-up-with-me."

"Why?" I sat on the bed. Her eyes were red from crying.

"He-was-gonna-ask-me-to-marry him."

"Really?"

"He told his mom, and she freaked out."

"I thought you said she liked you?"

"She seemed to."

I stroked her back. "You poor thing. But, why would he break up with you?"

"I don't know." She sobbed into her pillow. "I don't want to talk about it. Can you go away?"

"I'm sure he'll be back, Marianne. It's just a misunderstanding."

She sniffed. "Maybe."

The breakup had sent her into an emotional tailspin. She refused to eat, and she stood with her shoulders slumped and her pretty hair unkempt. She went to work, and her boss remarked on her less than professional appearance and fired her. Marianne had to stand in the unemployment line for hours as a result, which had been both humbling and depressing for her.

Mother was pragmatic about the ordeal, clucking, "Men. They're never around when you really need them. That's the one thing you can count on."

An old family friend, Mrs. Jennings, was back in town. She'd been to Italy with her sister, and now she wanted to see us again. We were invited to her house for dinner, but Marianne refused to go. Mrs. Jennings had outlived three husbands, all of whom had left her a great deal of money. She lived in style in a large house with a maid in the swanky part of town. Mom and I would go without Marianne, who preferred to pout in front of the computer, following Willoughby's movements via Twitter and Facebook.

As we left the apartment, Mr. Brandon was arriving.
"Hello, ladies."
"Hello, Mr. Brandon," said my mother. "How are you?"

He shrugged. "Fine. How's Marianne?"
"Miserable," I said.
"Maybe I'll stop by after I put these groceries away."

Mother brightened. "Do that. She needs to get away from the stupid computer."

"I'll see what I can do."

He was the best neighbor ever, and I held back the urge to hug him. He had tried repeatedly to get Marianne to go to the movies or dinner. I admired his determination and focus. He wasn't that much older than Marianne. She needed someone in her life who was mature and grounded. He was the obvious and sensible choice of a partner for her, but she was too blinded by false love to see that.

Mrs. Jennings had quite a few people over for dinner, which was surprising. Her gatherings were usually more intimate. We sat at a long table, surrounded by expensive dishes and shiny cutlery. The woman next to me was Lucy Steele. She was a friend of Mrs. Jennings daughter in law, and, as I listened to her, I felt sorry for her plight. Her parents had died years ago, one from cancer, the other from an infection. She'd been living with her older sister, but the arrangement had soured.

"Really, I'm so sick of this crappy economy. If I could get a full time job, I'd have health insurance."

"Times are tough for a lot of people," I said.

Mrs. Jennings interjected, "Lucy will be staying here for a few days."

Lucy was dark haired and pretty in a plain, yet sweet way. "I'm so grateful. I'll be looking for a job first thing tomorrow morning."

"Take your time, dear. There's no need to rush."

"Yes, but you've already done enough for me."

"Tosh. Don't worry about it."

Mrs. Jennings was an attractive woman with a trim, yet voluptuous body, which she'd always been proud of. She'd attracted her husbands with her charm and sex appeal, but now at fifty-four, she had resigned herself to the fact that her dating days were over.

"We're going shopping tomorrow, Lucy. Let's have some fun before you have to pound the pavement."

"I…okay."

Mother said, "What are you qualified to do, Ms. Steele?"

"Well, I've some college, and I worked for a dentist before. I'm good at organizing and data processing. I'll probably look for an office job or something."

We didn't have any openings where I worked. "If

you need help with your resume, let me know. I have a program that makes them look really good."

She smiled. "Thanks."

After dinner, Lucy and I settled on the sofa with glasses of wine and chatted for a long time about love and life.

She leaned in conspiratorially. "I actually have quite a secret."

My brows shot up. "You do?"

"Yes. I got married when I was sixteen."

"Is that allowed?"

"My parents were gone, and I was emancipated. I met this boy who was a little older. We were together one summer, and we hit it off. His family had money, and he felt bad for my situation. I have diabetes, and it's expensive." She looked wistful. "It was so romantic. We went to Reno and got married in one of those Chapel Of Love places. Then we came back to town and got an apartment. We never told anyone we'd gotten married."

"Where is your husband now?"

"Well, we realized after a while that we really didn't click. He was worried that his mom would raise hell, if she found out. She's a horrible woman." Her face scrunched up. "I never met her. She's made his life hell by controlling everything he does. I always wondered why he couldn't grow balls and tell her off."

This story was interesting. "Then what happened?"

"He gave me some money, and I went to live with my sister."

"How long have you been apart?"

"A long time."

"What if he wants to remarry? What if you find someone?"

She shrugged. "I don't know. Edward is shy. He's

never been that great with women, unless he's changed. I miss him sometimes, and I can't help wondering what would happen if I ever saw him again."

"Edward, huh?"

She whispered, "Yes, Edward Ferrars."

I nearly fell off my seat. Edward Ferrars was married! According to Ms. Steele, he had been married *forever*. That explained a few things. "Okay, wait a minute. Not to sound like a bitch, but why would someone stay married to someone, if they weren't even living together?"

"The health insurance. He has a great policy."

"What if you met a man and wanted to get married?"

Light flashed in her eyes. "Then I'd ask for a divorce."

"So, you're telling me that this guy is sacrificing himself by staying married to you?"

"I suppose if you want to look at it like that. He's never been all that great with women." She whispered, "He was a virgin when we were first…together. It wasn't even that good. If he really wanted to divorce, me, I wouldn't stop him."

This bit of news was astounding. "People do weird things."

She looked slightly offended by that statement. "He's trying to help me. I lost my parents; I lost everything. He wanted to help me; he still does."

I manufactured the most realistic smile I could. "I'm sorry. Of course, he put you first. It's really admirable, actually."

"Most men wouldn't do that. They'd walk away from a promise, if it became a hardship. But, I look at it this way. He lives his life, I live mine, and it works."

I took a sip of my drink, feeling like the bottom had

just dropped out of my stomach. "Yep, I guess."
	Later that night, I crawled into bed, wrapped the covers around me and cried.

Chapter Four

Just when Marianne was beginning to crawl out of her hole of depression, Mrs. Jennings invited us to the city for the week. An artist friend of hers was having a showing, and she wanted Marianne and I to attend. Mother looked forward to getting out of the condo, especially after new neighbors moved in and played the stereo full blast late into the night. My younger sister, Meggy, went to stay at a friend's house.

Marianne seemed suspiciously eager to get to the city, and, as we rode in the back of the car, I leaned into her. "What's going on?"

"What?"

"You seem weird."

"I'm fine."

"You don't even like Mrs. Jennings that much."

"She's all right."

I wondered at her demeanor. Something was up, but I would have to wait to find out what it was, because Marianne wasn't budging an inch.

Mrs. Jennings' apartment was decorated with antique furniture, thick carpets, and oil paintings of landscapes and still lifes.

My mother gave her a hug. "It's so good to see you again."

"I do love your family, honey. We'll have lots of fun this week. I want to take you to my favorite museums and the park. I have reservations for dinner tomorrow night at the best restaurant in town. It'll be such fun."

She'd set out an assortment of food, and we ate in the kitchen, which was a marvel of heavy wood and granite. One of her three cats darted in and out under the table, rubbing itself against my leg. Later, I realized I had forgotten my toothbrush, and I went to find Mrs. Jennings to see if she had an extra one.

"Come in."

I'd knocked on her bedroom door. "I forgot my toothbrush."

"Oh, you silly thing." She had on a silk robe, which clung to her ample curves. "I have an extra one." Her bathroom was huge with a clawfoot bathtub and built in cabinets. She reached into a drawer. "Here you are."

"Thanks so much."

"Before you go, I wanted to ask you a few questions. I hope you don't think I'm prying."

She strolled past me and sat on a small sofa in the corner of the room. I sat next to her.

"What do you want to know?"

"Poor Marianne. What on earth happened? I've never seen her so unhappy."

"Her boyfriend broke up with her."

Mrs. Jennings' look was sympathetic. "She must've been in love with him, because she's just devastated."

"She was. I think the hardest part for her was the way he ended it out of the blue. One day they were going out and then the next he was gone. She was so sure he loved her."

"Men can be like that sometimes. They're hard to figure out."

You're telling me. I was hung up on someone who was not only hard to figure out, but married. *Ugh.*

"I've learned a few things over the years. Never be entirely dependent on a man. It's wise to stand up on your own and take care of yourself."

That was easy for her to say, after she married three men and gotten their life insurance policies and bank accounts. If I had that much money, I'd be able to take care of myself too. I tamped down the monster of jealously.

She leaned in a fraction. "I do so admire you, honey. You've kept your mother sane by supporting her. The divorce left her shattered...and now he's gone. She loved him so."

"My dad had his flaws, but he was a good guy. I'm not fond of the bitch he married."

"Yes, she's a greedy one." Her gaze rested on my chest. "How are you? Is there anyone special in your life?"

The look in her eye affected me peculiarly. It was slightly predatory and...hungry? "Um, I'm doing okay."

"You aren't dating anyone right now?"

I shook my head.

"You're such a pretty girl. I can't believe you haven't married or had children yet."

I'd been too busy taking care of mother. "Not yet."

"But you won't close the door on the possibility, will you?"

That was a strange question. "No."

Her hand grazed my leg. "I wondered if, perhaps, you preferred the company of women."

I gasped, "No!"

Her smile was saucy. "I've had many lovers, honey, and not all of them were men."

Oh, my God! She's making a pass at me!

"I'm sorry I shocked you. I've always found you attractive, Elinor." Her hand was now on my thigh. My thin nightgown was no barrier to the heat of her hand. "Sometimes, when men aren't around...I like to have fun in other ways."

Should I leave now? Her hand massaged me in gentle, seductive strokes, making me tingle in my nether regions, which was strange. I'd never had sex with a woman before, mostly because they did not turn me on.

She grinned slyly. "You wouldn't have to do anything you're not comfortable with. I love…I love a pussy. They're so soft and wet. I could make you feel really good, Elinor."

I must have been giving her the wrong impression by staying and letting her hand stroke my thigh. I'd be lying, if I said it didn't feel nice. My body had begun to hum with sexual expectation, and the last time I had felt this type of lust had been with Edward.

"I'm not really into women."

"Of course not. I'm not asking you to make a lifestyle change. I'm just suggesting we…pleasure each other. Everyone is asleep. They'll never know."

The naughty insinuation in her voice had me tingling even worse now. She opened her robe, exposing huge breasts that were surprisingly high and firm. She'd never had children, so her body hadn't been ravaged by pregnancy. The sight of those vast globes with hard nipples surrounded by dark brown skin, made my sex clench. She noted my reaction, because her pupils dilated.

"I think you're on my wavelength now, aren't you?"

"We…I guess…"

"You should touch them. I want you to feel them."

Reaching out, I rubbed a jiggling mound, marveling at how warm it felt.

"Oh, yes," she hissed through her teeth. "Feel them."

I cupped a breast and held its weight in my hand, which was substantial. Then I pressed them together and leaned in to kiss one. Mrs. Jennings relaxed against the sofa while I buried my face in the soft cushions of her boobs, enjoying the sweet smell of her body.

"Yes. That's it. Suck a nipple, Elinor."

I drew a little nub into my mouth and sucked it to a stiff peak. Then I performed the task on the other, until it was just as wet and hard. I'd never done that to a woman before, and it had been incredibly arousing. She was so soft and warm, her body trembling ever so slightly. Feeling emboldened, I kissed her stomach, while sliding from the sofa to the carpet below. Her tummy wasn't toned; it was flat and lax, the skin jiggling faintly. Her thighs were also on the soft side, and, as I kissed them, she gasped.

"Oh, Elinor. That's wonderful."

She opened her thighs exposing her pussy, which I was surprised to find devoid of hair. Her labia was uneven around the edges and loose. She smelled slightly musky, with the light scent of whatever lotion she used on her body. Never having been this close to another woman's vagina, I was unsure about how to proceed.

Her fingers dipped into her pussy, as she stroked herself. "Don't be shy. You can lick me all you want."

What if I hated it? What if it made me gag? I felt a moment of hesitation, and then, as she continued to finger herself, I replaced her hand with my own, feeling her wetness.

"Oh, yes..."

Her head rested on the sofa; her chin was up, and her lips were slightly parted. Those massive breasts quivered ever so slightly, while her chest rose and fell with each breath. Conquering my fear, I settled between her thighs and approached her mound, which smelled even more pungent now due to her arousal. Wetness glistened around her opening, and, as I inserted a finger into the small, dark hole, she moaned. I wiggled it around for a moment until driving it in further.

"Oh, God, Elinor, that's it. Keep doing that."

It dawned on me that I was going to have to

commit to eating her out, or get up, make my apologies and leave. As she moaned and writhed beneath my finger, I'd made up my mind. Pulling apart her pussy flaps, I ran my tongue up the length of the slit, coating it in saliva.

"Yes!"

Her clit was small and hidden beneath the folds. The more I prodded it, the bigger it grew. This was a mildly fascinating phenomenon and spurred me on to play with it more, while I continued to dip my finger into her. Her breathing became uneven and ragged, while her moans filled the otherwise silent room. I was grateful that her bedroom was on the other side of the apartment. The last thing I needed was for my family to find out about my little lesbian escapade.

I let my tongue flatten out as I laved her clit. I could tell she was getting close to climax from the pressure her hands were applying on top of my head. She practically pushed my face into her wetness. I was coated with her musky odor, but I was determined to make her cum.

"Oh! Dear...shit...yes!" Her tummy began to convulse, and her thighs shook. She groaned loudly then, and moaned. "Elinor! Oh, God, yes! Fuck me!"

I'd made a woman orgasm. That thought was strange, yet exciting.

Chapter Five

"Oh, honey," she breathed. "That was so nice. It's my turn to make you feel good."

I needed a towel to wipe my face off. I was wet with her pussy juice. "I'll be right back." In the bathroom, I stared at myself and wondered who the hell this woman was in the mirror. My shoulder length dark hair was messy, and my brown eyes were bright. I always thought my features were plain, but tonight I looked different. My cheeks were flushed, my skin seemed to glow, and I fought a grin. I was single after all, and there was nothing wrong with a single woman having a little fun, was there?

In the bedroom, Mrs. Jennings was waiting for me. She had a black dildo in her hand, which made me catch my breath. I knew what she was going to do with that. The wetness in my panties was evidence to the fact that I had enjoyed eating her out and hearing her moan in completion. The night was hardly over.

"I have some things I want to do to you, Elinor."

That statement sent shivers up my spine. "Okay."

"Get on the bed, darling."

I grasped my nightgown and pulled it over my head. "I will." Then I got on the bed, shivering ever so slightly out of nervousness and excitement. Mrs. Jennings' voluptuous, naked form approached, and I admired her breasts, because they truly were magnificent. They were like soft pillows that I wanted to bury myself in. Perhaps, she would let me do it again later?

"Now, lay back, and relax." She drew near, touching my breasts gently and caressing the skin. "You're so beautiful, Elinor. I've always been attracted to you."

That statement was a shocker. "Really?"

"I've had a feeling about you. I know you prefer men, but I knew you'd like this too." Her hand drifted to my stomach where she massaged me. "There's nothing wrong with seeking pleasure from the same sex when men aren't available." She smiled slightly. "I have to tell you. My last husband liked to have threesomes. That's how this all got started for me. He'd bring home women, and we...well, we'd have sex together. That's where I learned that I loved to have a woman eating my pussy. It feels so good."

"I had no idea."

"Of course not. It was our dirty little secret." Her hand was over my pussy, rubbing within the folds. "Is this nice? Do you like it?"

"I...yes."

She giggled, "Good. I can't wait to fuck you, honey."

That sent a pleasure chill through me, and I waited for her, as she settled between my thighs. Her finger had yet to leave my slit, and she worked it up and down, stroking and provoking my clit. Her hot breath fanned out seconds before she drove into my hole with a purposeful thrust, which had me gasping.

I'd only ever experienced this with a man, so the feel of a woman, the softness, the gentleness, was a delightful surprise. Her tongue was deep in my hole, laving and seducing me. I stared at the ceiling, marveling at how wonderful this was and not wanting it to end. With a man, there was far more saliva and the scratchy effects of a beard. She was so soft, yet persistent, and that tongue seemed to twitter and twirl inside of me, rubbing the inner walls of my tunnel. She sucked the fluid out of me, catching every last drop of my desire, and, when I thought I couldn't take it anymore, she withdrew and rubbed the end of the dildo against me.

"Do you like a black cock?"

That was so naughty. "Yes."

"I love sex toys. I can't live without them."

"Me either," I moaned.

The dildo stroked me repeatedly, coating in my juices. Then she began to insert it bit by bit, only to pull it out again and rub it up and down. She was doing exactly what I did at home with my toys, and I knew this would be good. The slight penetration and then the prodding of my clit had me grasping the sheets and arching my back.

"Oh, ooohh…"

"Yes, that's it. Take that cock, you dirty girl."

The black sex toy was now burrowing in deeper with each stroke. She withdrew it and brought it to her mouth and sucked on it while I watched.

"Yum. You taste like sex."

That was so dirty. I had no idea Mrs. Jennings was such a naughty girl. She smiled and pushed the cock into me, until I could feel it in my stomach. Pulling it out, she let it slide up to my clit where it inflamed the little nub to an erotic fever pitch.

"You should lean over the bed."

"What?"

"I want to fuck you harder, Elinor."

"I…okay."

She laughed, "Don't you trust me? Don't you want it hard and fast now? I can work you like a man. Would you like that?"

I shivered pleasurably. "Yes."

"Good. Now get that ass off the bed and lean over. Mommy wants to fuck you." I did as instructed, offering her my backside, while she stood behind me. "Are you ready, honey?"

"Yes."

"Good. Now relax, and I'll have you screaming in no time."

That statement was not an exaggeration. As the toy plunged into my hungry orifice, she worked it in and out with controlled persistence that had me gasping into the sheets and gripping them with my fingertips. The sound of hot, wet sex filled the room as the dildo fucked me repeatedly. She seemed to know exactly how far to push without crossing the line. I arched my back, anticipating each intrusion and welcoming it with every cell in my body.

"You dirty girl, Elinor. Fuck that cock, you dirty girl."

"Ooohh…God…"

"Yes. That's it. This is making me so horny. You'll have to fuck me like this next. We should do this all night."

"Oh, Mrs. Jennings!"

"That's it. You're very close."

A wet, squashing sound filled the room along with my gasps of pleasure. With each thrust, the instrument hit something wonderful that had me trembling and moaning. As the first inkling of release beckoned, I moaned loudly, not caring if the entire house heard it. The orgasm slammed into me with such force, I bit my lip as I convulsed and throbbed around the dildo, which was being hammered into me almost brutally.

"Good girl. That's it. Ride it out."

She continued to fuck me as the last dregs of satisfaction drained from my body, leaving me as relaxed and limp as a wet rag.

The next morning, after Mrs. Jennings and I had made ourselves cum several more times, I was exhausted, yet more relaxed then I could ever remember being. We hit the town for a shopping trip, and mother got her hair done at a salon, while Mrs. Jennings spoiled Marianne and me with new clothes. After having had lunch, we came back to the apartment and relaxed until it was time to go to dinner and the art gallery.

Marianne wore a black satin dress, and her hair was in a loose bun, which made her look adorable. She beamed with happiness. All day she had been acting strange.

"What's going on?" We were in a taxi on the way to the venue.

"What do you mean?"

"You seem super happy."

She sighed. "I am."

"Are you going to let me in on your little secret?"

"I might've found out that Willoughby is in town. There's a chance he'll be at the show."

"Has he called you?"

"No. I've been following him on Twitter."

"Oh." I worried that she was getting her hopes up, only to have them crushed. "You should be careful, sweetie. Don't get too excited about this. If he wanted to be with you, he'd—"

"Be quiet!" she snapped. "All he has to do is see me again, and he'll remember why he loves me. I don't want to talk about this." She stared out the window, giving me the profile of her pretty face.

I sat back in the seat. "Fine." I feared she was heading for a massive let down.

The art gallery was packed, and the smell of a dozen or more perfumes mingled in the air. Mrs. Jennings knew quite a few people, and we were taken around and introduced. The artist in question wore white-rimmed eyeglasses and a strange crinkled, green dress. She spoke with a high-pitched nasal quality that had me wincing with each word. Her work was what I could only describe as strange. Most of the paintings were darkly colored, with only tiny patches of paint in them. I had no idea why everyone seemed to be drooling over them, and, as I reached for another glass of wine, my stomach dropped.

Mr. Willoughby had just entered with a tall, thin looking woman on his arm. I glanced over at Marianne to see if she'd just witnessed this, and from the shocked, drained expression on her face, she had. *Oh, crap!*

She cut a path through the room to reach him, and I heard her say, "Fancy meeting you here. How are you?"

He stared at her, as if he'd seen a ghost. His date glared at Marianne, and then she focused that stringent look on him.

"Um, hello, Marianne. How are you?"

"I've been wanting to talk to you. Do you think we could have a moment?"

His date's mouth opened, and, just as she was about to speak, Mr. Willoughby said, "I'm sorry. I…that won't be possible. Excuse me." He guided her to the other side of the room, where they engaged in a heated discussion.

I reached Marianne just in time to see her sway unsteadily on her feet. Her eyes were filled with tears. "Let's get outta here."

"Yes," she sniffed.

In the taxi, she succumbed to tears, and I held her while she cried. "It's gonna be okay," I whispered. "Fuck him. He's a moron anyway."

Chapter Six

Being rejected by Willoughby sent Marianne into an emotional tailspin. While Mrs. Jennings and I went out to lunch the next day, Marianne stayed in bed, refusing to talk to anyone.

"That poor girl," murmured Mrs. Jennings. "I've heard that he's going to marry that woman. She's quite a catch. Her father's a hedge fund manager, and he's worth billions."

"Well, that explains a few things."

To my surprise, I recognized Lucy Steele at the next table. She waved to me, then dropped her napkin and came over.

"Hello, Elinor." She grinned. "How are you?"

"I'm good, and you?" I wondered who the man was she was sitting with.

"Terrific. Hi, Mrs. Jennings."

"Hello, dear."

"I'm having lunch with Robert Ferrars, Edward's brother. I'm staying at the Palmer's for a while. They know the Ferrars."

I felt a twinge of jealousy. She would get to spend time with Edward, no doubt. "It's nice that they let you stay with them."

"I might have a job here. I have another interview tomorrow."

"Well, good for you," said Mrs. Jennings.

Lucy smiled politely. "Thanks. How long will you be in the city?"

"This week. I'm staying with Mrs. Jennings." I nodded to my lunch partner.

"Maybe we can get together?"

"I'll give you my number." I scribbled it on a napkin.

She smiled. "Thanks."

She went back to her table and engaged in an animated conversation with Mr. Robert Ferrars. Knowing now that he was Edward's brother, I could see the similarities, but I much preferred the way Edward looked. Robert had a clear overbite and a double chin. Unfortunately, he'd gotten the short end of the genetic stick.

"She seems like a nice girl."

She's married to the man I love. Ugh. "Yeah. She's nice." My lunch was ruined, but I tried to plaster a smile on my face and power through, even though my heart was breaking. I had to try to let him go. I was clinging to him just as stupidly as Marianne clung to Willoughby.

We spent the evening at the apartment, and Mrs. Jennings and I played *Scrabble*, while Marianne was on the computer, cyberstalking Willoughby, no doubt.

"Oh, my God," said Marianne. "That bastard's going to marry her! She's a totally rich bitch."

I glanced at Mrs. Jennings.

She closed her laptop. "Ugh."

"Her father's a billionaire, honey. You can't compete with that," said Mrs. Jennings. "There are lots of other men. Don't waste anymore time on him."

Marianne unplugged her computer and, without saying another word, left the room.

"That poor girl."

My mother suddenly appeared. "You'll never believe what I just heard. I got a call from Mrs. Palmer, and you remember Lucy Steele? That girl's been married to Edward for years, and his mother never know about it, until she spilled the beans last night."

I sat up, suddenly interested in this conversation. "Yeah?"

"Well, the family's in an uproar. You remember Edward's mother, right? She wants Edward to annul the marriage. She says it wasn't legal anyway, because Lucy was only sixteen. She's got lawyers working on it right now."

"So?"

"Well, Edward's out of a job. She had the board fire him as CEO. Robert's running the show now."

I rubbed my forehead. "Give me a break. Who does that?"

"That woman doesn't like Lucy Steele for some reason. She's an angry and vindictive bitch. So, unless Edward divorces or annuls her, he's no longer in the family business."

"Maybe he'll do that." Hope flared eternal, but then my mother spoke.

"No. He refuses. He feels obligated to Lucy, and he won't divorce her."

"That's just bizarre," said Mrs. Jennings. "So he marries this woman years ago, and he never told his family?"

I shook my head. It didn't make any sense to me either, but then again, I was hardly impartial.

Mother said, "Well, every family has its secrets. If you see him again, Elinor, you should ask him."

I muttered, "Doubt that will happen."

Yet, the next day, to my utter shock, Edward Ferrars of all people was at the door. I stared at him for a full minute in shock.

"I...found out from Lucy that you were here."

"Oh, yeah, right. Come in." My heart lodged itself in my throat. He was so lean and tall, his body filling in the space in the dimly lit entryway. I led him into the living room, where I sat on a sofa. "How've you been?"

He had faint circles under his eyes. "Shitty."

Wow. That was an honest answer. "I heard about your marriage to Lucy Steele." I smiled sheepishly. "Gossip spreads like fire, ya know?"

He nodded. "I've been married to her for a long time. It...was a mistake...but I didn't know how to get out of it."

"Is that why you don't date?"

He seemed surprised by the question. "I date, but I don't let it get serious." He looked troubled and uncomfortable. "I don't want to be married to her, but she needs health insurance. I could give her money, but it would only be temporary, cause she'd run out of it. She has diabetes, and it's expensive."

"I understand."

"When I met her she'd just lost her parents. I felt really protective of her, and I was pissed that the world had let her down. I wanted to help. I was kinda young and stupid. I know now that I can't save everyone I meet. It's not possible."

"Haven't you lost your job? What about the insurance?"

"I still have a job. I'm just not CEO anymore, and I really don't care."

"Don't you want your own life?"

His look was vague. "I do."

"But?"

"I...have to stand up to my mother. I'm worried about Lucy, but I don't think I can keep this charade up anymore. I need to be free. I shouldn't use this as an excuse not to go after what I want."

What do you want?

"Edward!" My mother had walked into the room.

"What are you doing here?" Surprise lit her eyes.

He stood. "Hello, Mrs. Dashwood. I heard you were here, so I stopped by."

"Well, isn't that nice. I have to confess; you're the only one of my ex-husband's family that I really like. The rest of 'em could fall off a pier for all I care."

"Mom!" God. How embarrassing.

"Well, it's true." She dared me to challenge her.

Edward smiled kindly. "I understand. More than you know."

"Will you stay for the day?"

"I can't. I have to go. I just wanted to stop by and see Elinor."

My mother's brows shot up. "Oh, really?" Her expression was calculating.

I shook my head at her, annoyed. "I'll walk you to the door."

"Say hi to Marianne and Meggy for me."

"I will."

In the entryway, I turned to stare at him, wishing he didn't have to leave so soon. I tingled everywhere, remembering our last encounter, which seemed like a lifetime ago.

He looked torn and sad.

"Are you okay?"

"I guess."

Impulse took over, and I hugged him. "Can I ask you something?" His face was in my neck, sending pleasurable chills down my spine.

"What?"

"Do you like me at all?"

His hands wrapped around my back, drawing me to him. "Yes." Hot breath was on my neck, and then he was kissing me, sucking at the delicate skin. "I like you a lot."

"I..." There were so many things I wanted to say to him. I had tons of questions, and, as frustrating as it was not being able to ask them, I let my mouth do the talking, kissing him senseless.

"God, Elinor."

His tongue was silky and persistent. We devoured each other, not caring that we might be observed. My sister was in her room, crying more than likely, and Mrs. Jennings was in the kitchen, making a peach cobbler. This moment was ours, and, if we had to steal it, then we would.

I pressed myself to him, feeling the hardness of his cock. Knowing he was as turned on as I was, I felt a moment of desperation. I had to have him. Grasping the nearest doorknob, I pulled open the closet and pushed him in.

He chuckled, "You're a wild woman, Ms. Dashwood."

"You have no idea."

The closet smelled of mothballs and leather, but I could have cared less. I undid his pants, letting his penis free. Dropping to my knees, I took him in my mouth until I gagged.

"Oh, God, yes..."

Fire flamed inside of me, spurring me on to take what was not mine, but not caring in the least. Inhaling his cock, I sucked on the rounded tip tasting his salty pre-cum. My panties were damp, and my pussy throbbed, wanting him inside of me. I unzipped my jeans and let them drop.

With my hands pressed to the wall, I gasped, "Take me."

Edward was behind me in a flash, his hot hands on my hip as he guided himself into my silken hole. With one long thrust he was buried deep.

"Ooohhh...fuck me..."

"I can't stop thinking of that night."

"Me either. Don't stop."

He began to plunge, filling me with that magnificent cock. Here we were in a coat closet having dirty sex against the wall, and it was the most thrilling thing ever. My married lover pounded me, gasping and moaning with each thrust, while my head knocked against the wall, producing small thumping sounds. My pussy throbbed around him, compressing and milking his shaft.

"Elinor!"

"Fuck me, Edward. Oh, God...I'm getting close."

I pressed my face to the wall, while he drove his cock in deep and withdrew only to sink in again. The sound of his balls slapping against me joined our mingled groans. I clung to the wall, as the first onslaught left me convulsing and trembling in repletion. He hammered me then, gasping and shouting my name.

"Elinor!"

My tunnel was filled with his hot spunk, as he squirted his seed in me. I wasn't on the pill, so I had a moment of concern, but I brushed it aside. He slid in and out, over and over, extracting the last dregs of pleasure from his orgasm.

He pressed me to the wall. "God."

"I wish we could do this more often."

His mouth was on my neck, kissing and biting gently. "I know."

Chapter Seven

The day we were supposed to go home, Marianne disappeared. She said she wanted to run to the corner store, but she never came back. For two days we worried about where she had gone, so much so, my mother contacted Mr. Brandon and asked him if he'd heard from her. He was so concerned, that he arrived within hours. On the third day, he'd found her shivering in an alleyway and sick. We met them at the hospital where Marianne was diagnosed with pneumonia.

I stood by her bed and gazed at her pale, exhausted face. She took my hand.

"I'm okay, Elinor. Don't look at me like that."

"You scared the shit outta us. Don't you ever do that again."

"I...won't."

"What the hell were you thinking anyway?"

"I had to see him again."

"Did you?"

"I watched his apartment. I watched him go in with *her*. Then I waited for hours until they came back out. I confronted him. I..." Tears were in her eyes. "I begged him to come back to me."

"Oh, Marianne."

She sniffed. "He wouldn't. He...doesn't love me."

I hugged her, mindful of the I.V. "You poor thing. He's moved on, the bastard."

"I know he loved me. I know he did."

"He has his own reasons for what he did, sweetie. We'll never know why he left like that."

She cried, "I hate men."

"You'll get over this, Marianne. It'll take a while,

but you can do this. I know you can."

When she was well enough to go home, we sat in Mrs. Jennings living room with Mozart playing softly and the smell of meatloaf in the oven. Mr. Brandon was next to Marianne on the sofa, and he held her feet on his lap. They made a cute couple, and I hoped that once my sister had recovered from her illness and her heartbreak, she would wake up and see that the perfect man was already in her life.

Mrs. Jennings strolled into the room. "Dinner should be done soon. I got a call from Mrs. Palmer. I have news, girls. Interesting news."

I glanced at her. "What?"

"I heard that Ms. Steele has been accepted into the Ferrars family with open arms."

I felt sick.

"I guess that mean and nasty mother had a change of heart."

Getting to my feet, I said, "Excuse me." I had to be alone. I didn't want to hear anymore. I sat on my bed and stared at the wall. My door opened a second later.

"What's wrong, Elinor?" Marianne sat next to me.

"Nothing."

"Don't say it's nothing. You're clearly upset."

"I…like Edward. I've always liked him."

She put her arm around me. "He's married to Lucy. It sounds like the family has accepted it."

"Yeah."

"Does he love her?"

"How the hell do I know?"

"What's wrong with that family? Are they bipolar?" Marianne giggled at her own joke.

"I don't think he loves her. He married her when he was young. She was only sixteen."

"Why would he stay in a marriage like that?"

"She's got diabetes. She needs medical insurance."

Understanding shone in her clear blue eyes. "Oh."

"He's done the honorable thing."

She snorted. "I guess."

I glanced at her.

"Come on. Couldn't he find a way out? I mean, she could've gotten Medicaid or something. He didn't have to be responsible. It's not his problem."

"He's a good person, Marianne. He wanted to help."

She slumped. "I don't get that. Why saddle yourself with someone, just cause they can't take care of themselves."

"People do all kinds of things that make no sense."

"Like Willoughby just leaving like that. One day we were so in love and then the next, poof. He's gone."

"You should hook up with Mr. Brandon. He likes you."

"I guess. I'm not feeling the passion and the fireworks with him."

"Maybe you have something deeper going on? It isn't all about the fireworks, you know?"

"That's Elinor, being sensible. I like passion. I like losing my mind in love."

"Maybe that will develop with him? You never know. You're still pining for Willoughby. Once that finally wears off, you might see things differently."

She shrugged.

The next morning, I waited on the sidewalk with the luggage, while mother said goodbye to our kind hostess. A taxi pulled up, and the door opened revealing Edward! He paid the driver and headed towards me with a huge smile on his face. My mouth fell open.

"Hi."

"Hi."

"I caught you just in time."

"We...we're leaving."

"I can see that."

Did he have to look so good? The breeze brought his cologne over, and it teased my senses, making my pussy throb. "Congratulations on everything."

"What?"

"On Lucy and your family. I heard she's been accepted."

He looked confused. "No, I mean, yes. She's been welcomed, but...you haven't heard?"

"Heard what?"

"She's engaged to my brother. They met a couple of weeks ago and hit it off. My mother's lawyers managed to get my marriage annulled and..." he laughed soundly, "and then she snags my brother."

"I thought your mother hated her?"

"Lucy's like the tick on a dog's ass that won't let go. My brother's mad about her."

This family had issues. "Okay."

"I've been reinstated as CEO, and I've been forgiven. I told her about you. I told her that I was going to ask you to marry me." He smiled. "She's pissed, but she'll get over it."

I was so shocked; words failed me.

"You wouldn't mind marrying me, would you?" He pulled out an item from his jacket pocket. "I came prepared." He opened a black velvet box, producing a sparkling diamond ring. "This was my grandmother's. It's probably not your style at all, but you can have it changed or whatever." His grin was huge. "What do you say, Elinor? You wanna shack up with me, or what?"

I flung myself at him. "I can't believe this." Happiness filled my heart to bursting. "This isn't happening."

His face was in my neck. "Yeah, it is."

Two weeks later, we were married, and Marianne and Mr. Brandon were dating, albeit cautiously. My mother was so thrilled by my marriage; she dyed her hair red and promptly got a boyfriend who was ten years younger. As our fortunes improved and our lives changed, it occurred to me I had the best of both worlds. I'd ended up with a sensible choice for a husband, but he was also wildly passionate in bed, and, maybe one day, I would tell him about my fling with Mrs. Jennings, or not.

The End

Naughty Emma

Chapter One

The sound of the PA system woke me from a deep, dream-filled sleep. My father's croaky voice said, "Good morning. Welcome to another season at Camp Highbury. The staff meeting is at 0600 hours. Time to get up and get 'em. See you there!"

"Ugh." I rolled over and nearly fell out of the single bed. Why did I put myself through this every summer? I'd just graduated from college, and I should be job hunting, not mucking around again in the wilderness getting eaten by mosquitos and bled dry by ticks.

"It's only five thirty," moaned my cabinmate.

I had met Harriet Smith yesterday. We had taken the same boat in along with several counselors I hadn't met before. Daddy had to hire new staff every season. A few returned, but many did not.

"Ah...the joy." It had rained last night, and the damp wood smelled like urine. Nothing said camp like the smell of a backed up latrine. "I hope they put coffee on. I'm gonna need it."

Harriet's brown hair looked like it had been caught in a windstorm. "He'd probably cut you some slack for being his daughter, Emma."

I threw my leg over the side of the bed. "Nope. No such luck." I had to use the bathroom. "Be back in a sec." As I stepped into my sneakers, I prayed there weren't any spiders under the toilet seat. When I returned, Harriet had made her bed and dressed. I opened a creaky cabinet door and chose my clothing for the day, which all smelled like rotting wood now.

When we were ready, Harriet and I left the cabin and stepped out into the cool morning. A thin mist hung over the lake and the beachfront. As soon as the sun appeared over the distant mountain, the moisture would evaporate, and things would warm up considerably.

"There are some cute lifeguards," said Harriet.

She had confided to me yesterday that she was single. "Oh, for sure. The waterfront instructors are always the hottest, that and the outdoor education people. You won't be single for long."

Harriet snorted. "Ha! I have crap luck with guys. Don't hold your breath."

I glanced at her through my lashes. "I'm pretty good at playing match maker. Last season I got the climbing instructor, Mr. Weston, and a hospitality staff member together. I got them in the same canoe and left them without oars. Four hours later, they were dating." A self-satisfied smug left me beaming with pride. "If you want, I could work my magic again. Just tell me which guy you like, and I'll see what I can do."

"You're crazy."

"No, seriously. I have skills. Don't underestimate a Woodhouse."

"I'll try to remember that."

We were on a path heading to the Bear Lodge. Other staff members began to emerge, looking tired, yet eager to meet our new camp guests. Camp Highbury was coed, catering to teen boys and girls.

"I'll hook you up in no time."

"What about you?"

"Me?"

"Don't you want a boyfriend?"

The thought of hooking up with a staff member

was repulsive. I wasn't interested in little boys. My sights were set on successful men who had jobs and nice cars. "Um...I'm good. I don't have time to date right now."

We'd reached the lodge, which filled up quickly with an assortment of employees. Daddy had on a pair of reading glasses, and he squinted at a handheld clipboard. I recognized a family friend, Mr. George Knightly. His brother was married to my sister. For some bizarre reason, he liked to help us every season as Camp Supervisor. He spoke with a gorgeous brunette I'd never seen before. I approached him, eager to find out who the statuesque beauty was.

"Emma!" His gray eyes brightened when he saw me. "How are you?"

"Fantastic." I glared at the woman. "Hi."

She held out her hand. "Hello. I'm Jane. Jane Fairfax."

I shook her hand. "Emma. Are you on the arts staff?"

"No. I'm a nurse."

"Oh."

"Emma's the director's daughter," clarified George.

Jane's brows shot up. "I see."

She smiled kindly, but I felt pings of irritation. I'd never admit this openly, but I was horribly prideful about my looks. It was necessary that I be the prettiest in a room, which I frequently was. With my long, blonde hair, cornflower blue eyes, and perfectly proportioned features, I turned heads wherever I went. This Jane person was a serious challenge...and I did not like that one bit.

"Daddy seems to be hiring them older this year."

Mr. Knightley's mouth fell open. "Emma!"

"I mean, more experienced."

Jane and George exchanged a look, which I

ignored.

Harriet was talking to someone across the room. He wore a white apron. Ugh. No! The kitchen staff was strictly off limits where dating was concerned. "Excuse me." I cut a path through the throng to save her from forming an attachment to whomever she was chatting up.

"Welcome everyone," said daddy. "It's our twenty-fifth season here at Camp Highbury. Welcome new staff members and old. At eight a.m. sharp, your charges will arrive. I'll be passing out the activities packet. Please look it over, and double check that you're listed in the correct places. Any screw ups need to be fixed immediately."

I tapped Harriet on the shoulder. She turned around, smiling.

"Emma, I want you to meet Robert Martin. He's the head cook. He says we can sneak food out of the fridge anytime."

I eyed him, finding him less than appealing. He was pockmarked and rough looking. "How nice." I pulled Harriet away, whispering, "Oh, God no. Don't waste your time on him. There are some hot guys here." I steered her through the crowd, while daddy talked to the new arrivals. "Now, there's someone interesting." I pointed to a tall, dark haired man, wearing a pair of khaki shorts and a polo shirt. As we approached, I bumped into his elbow. "Oh, I'm so sorry."

He grinned. "That's all right."

"I...don't remember you from last year."

"I wasn't here."

"I'm Emma, and this is Harriet." I stood back, so he could get a good view of my friend.

"Hi. I'm Philip Elton."

"Where are you from, Philip?" I asked.

"Maine."

He wore thick leather sandals, a neatly pressed shirt, and a stainless steel Rolex. *Oooh! He screams potential.*

"Well, lucky for us you chose to work at Camp Highbury this summer. I'm sure we'll get to know each other a lot better before the season is over."

He grinned. "I hope so."

After the meeting, Harriet and I made a beeline for the arts building to make sure all of our supplies had arrived. She had been hired for woodworking, and I was teaching creative arts and landscaping. She showed me some of the projects she had completed, and I was impressed.

On our way back to the lodge to meet the new arrivals, Ms. Bates stopped me. She was on the janitorial staff, and I'd known her for years.

"Miss Woodhouse!"

"Hi. How are you?"

"I'm good. It's so nice to see you again."

"I know. Crazy, huh? Another summer and here we are."

"I always look forward to working here. It's a nice break from the factory, and the wages are better."

Why someone would want to keep working at crappy jobs was beyond me. "Gotta get ready for the kids. See ya."

She waved. "Good luck."

"Thanks."

An hour later, pandemonium erupted with the influx of eager, noisy campers. Each and every staff member was needed on the first day to help the kids find their cabins, give tours of the grounds, and deal with any last minute emergencies. I'd been grouped with Philip Elton, and, as we shepherded the new comers to their various cabins, I found out that he was a recent Harvard grad, which raised him dramatically in my estimation. He would be perfect for Harriet.

Chapter Two

That night at dinner, I made sure Philip was seated nearby with Harriet on one side and I on the other. George was across from us, and I tried to ignore him. His expression was considering and a touch judgmental, which I found annoying.

"Philip went to Harvard, Harriet."

She chewed on her steak, her jaw working. "Um...nice."

"He was captain of his lacrosse team."

"Oh, wow."

"He's the Canoe Trip Leader." Did Harriet have to chew like that? "Maybe you could give us a tour of the boathouse later?"

He grinned. "I'd love to."

George crossed his arms over his chest and stared at me. Why he wasn't married yet was a mystery. He'd been engaged and close to marriage, but he'd called it off at the last second. He had to be approaching forty, at least, or maybe he was younger than that.

"So, what do you do, Harriet?" asked Philip conversationally.

"I worked at a discount warehouse for a while. I was in school."

"Which school?"

"Community college."

He nodded. "Some of us got our start there."

"It was good while it lasted. I kinda didn't know what major was, so I quit."

"You're in woodworking, right?"

"Yeah. I like it, but it's not really a job. It's more a hobby."

"She makes amazing totem poles," I said. "You should see them. Her carvings are really good. Her squirrels are totally lifelike."

Mr. Knightley rubbed the space between his eyes. If he was bored with the conversation, he was more than welcome to sit elsewhere.

"Awesome. I'll have to check it out. How about you, Emma? Which school did you go to?"

"I went to one in Massachusetts."

"There are a couple good ones there," murmured Philip.

I shrugged. I wasn't going to reveal my school. "You love watersports, don't you, Harriet?"

"Oh, for sure."

"I learned to waterski a couple of years ago. Do you waterski, Philip?"

"A little."

The conversation at dinner left me exhausted because I had to consciously keep it flowing. Whenever there had been a pause, I filled it in with anything that popped into my head. Harriet was the worst at making small talk.

George came up behind me as I poured lemonade into my glass.

"That was quite a show."

"What?"

"At dinner."

"What do you mean?"

"He's not interested in her, Emma. I don't know why you're bothering."

"Ouf. Go away."

He laughed, "Nothing ever changes with you. Why don't you manage your own life, instead of sorting out everyone else's?"

"That's rich, coming from you."

"What do you mean by that?"

"Just because your brother married my sister doesn't mean you have to hang around. Why don't you go off on some Buddhist sabbatical and chant or something."

Anger flashed in his eyes. "I happen to like your family, you little shit. I *hang* around because I admire your dad and I love this camp."

If he could be angry, then so could I. "I want Harriet to have a nice summer. What's wrong with her dating Mr. Elton for a little while? There's nothing wrong with a summer fling."

"He's not into her; that's why. He's more into you."

I brushed that aside. "No. He just needs the proper encouragement. I think they'd make a great couple. There's no reason for you to stick your nose in my business." Those intense gray eyes were on me.

"I'm sure Harriet is perfectly capable of finding her own boyfriend."

"No, she isn't. I've had success at getting people together. After I'm done working my magic, they'll be all over each other like a rash."

"Poison ivy?"

I smirked at him. "Goodbye, George."

"Goodbye, Ms. Woodhouse."

Later that night, Harriet, Philip, and I were in the boathouse, which smelled faintly of fish. The water lapped against the wood in the boat bay. Philip had produced a bottle of wine and poured it into paper cups. I was slightly drunk and giggly. We sat in the corner, and Harriet and I wrapped a wool, army blanket around us.

"I like being bad at camp," said Philip. "We should do something naughty."

"Like what?"

"You girls should kiss."

I sucked in a breath. "No."

"Why not? That would be so hot."

"How about I kiss you?" asked Harriet, suddenly emboldened.

"There's an idea."

Harriet let go of the blanket and crawled over to Philip. "Okay, here goes."

She planted a big wet one on him. They kissed for long minutes while I watched. I could hear people laughing in the distance, and I worried they might stumble upon us. It was wonderful that Harriett was getting to know Philip better. Everything was going exactly to plan.

Mr. Elton gasped, "How about you suck my cock?"

I thought Harriet would slap him, but instead, she smirked. "Oh, yeah? Show us what it looks like."

Whoa. This had gone from zero to sixty awfully fast. Before I was able to say anything, Philip zipped his shorts down, exposing a pale, hard cock. Harriet was on it in a flash, sucking on the engorged end like a seasoned pro.

"Yeah, that's so nice. Suck me, baby."

Harriet glanced at me. "You should help. We can work him together."

This suggestion was a shock. I'd only had sex with two people, both of whom I had fancied myself in love with. The thought of performing oral sex on a complete stranger repulsed me. The fact that Harriet would do so was an unpleasant revelation and a reflection on her character, or lack there of. Was she drunk? She had to be drunk.

"Um, I'm good. I'll just hang or do you want me to leave?"

"No," said Philip. "You should stay and watch this dirty girl suck my cock."

The sound of her sloppy, wet sucks filled the boathouse. A window above my head let the light from the moon shine in. I could plainly see her running her tongue up and down his tool.

"Yeah, that's it. Suck it."

She grabbed him. "What else can you do with this thing?"

"I could fuck you with it."

"Ohh...that would be sooo dirty."

"I can give it to you nasty, if that's what you want."

Without a second's hesitation, Harriet pulled her shorts down and got on her hands and knees with her bare bum in the air. "Show me what you got, Mr. Elton. Fuck me."

He was on her in a flash, touching her cheeks. "I like a nice fat ass."

Harriet gasped. "It's not!"

He smacked her. "Oh, yes it is. Just the way I like 'em." He grinned at me. "Your friend is a hot one."

I was speechless. They were about to have sex right then and there. "Are you sure you want to do this, Harriet?"

"Ooohh...yeah. Fuck me, Philip. Do it."

He knelt behind her and prodded her with his cock, which looked enormous. With one push, he was buried deep. "Oh, God."

"Oh, that's it. It's so big." She dropped her head, letting her hair fall in her face. "Fuck me hard. I love it hard."

Watching them was turning me on, but not enough to join them. My pussy dripped with arousal, so my panties were damp. I'd never seen anyone having sex before, and these two had all but forgotten I was there. They groaned and moaned their bliss, while Philip pounded her from behind. The boathouse had begun to smell of hot, pungent sex.

"Oh, I love it! Fuck me. I'm getting close."

"You dirty little whore." He drove himself into her, his balls smashing against her. "This is how sluts get fucked."

"Arrgg...all...shit...yes! It's so good!" She convulsed around him, shuddering and mumbling incoherently. "Ooohh..."

He pulled himself free. "Suck it, bitch. Make me cum."

Harriett ate him up and gagged, while rubbing his wet meat with her fingertips. It looked even bigger than before, and I marveled at how much of it she got down her throat. She was really good at this.

He groaned then and pulled himself out of her mouth. "Oh, yeah, that's it. Open up you little whore, and eat my cum."

Harriett waited with her tongue out, and, a second later, he groaned, while white cream sprayed over her forehead into her hair. Subsequent spurts landed in her mouth and near her lips. She sucked him down her throat, cleaning the shaft thoroughly.

Someone cleared his throat behind us. I turned to find Mr. Knightley. *Oh, shit!*

Chapter Three

"I'd like to talk to you, Emma."

Oh, God. How embarrassing! My cheeks flamed. It was like getting caught naked by the entire football team. I got to me feet and went to him, not daring to look at Harriet. She had cum all over her face. George's posture was tense, his jaw was set, and his arms swung stiffly at his sides.

We walked towards the recreation center, and he unlocked a side door, letting me pass by him. It was dark within the large open space, save for a security light at the back.

He turned to me. "What the hell was that?"

"Look, you're not my father. I'm a grown woman. I...can do whatever I want."

Anger sparked in his eyes. "This is a camp with a bunch of kids! What if one of them had walked in on you? We could all go to jail on sex charges! I can't believe you did that."

I was indignant. "I didn't do anything! They were doing it. I didn't know Harriet was going to have sex with him. We were having wine...and—"

"Now you're telling me there's booze too? This is a dry camp. We could get into a shitload of trouble, if anybody found out there was booze."

"Oh, for Christ's sake. We didn't share it with the freaking campers. Stop over reacting to everything."

"You've been out of control since I met you."

"What's that supposed to mean?"

"Shopping, partying, and drugging. God only knows what other shit you've done."

I faced him with my hands on my hips. "You got

some nerve, George. I never did drugs. Before you accuse me of stuff, you better get your damn facts straight!"

He pointed a finger in my face. "Your father should've tightened the lead a long time ago. You're a spoiled brat in the worst sense."

I gasped and slapped him. "Get a life, George! Go get your own damn family. Stop sucking off us. Quit being a loser."

The look in his eye should have been a warning. He grabbed me, pulled me onto his lap on the sofa, and spanked me. I had a moment where I wasn't sure this was actually happening to me.

"You need to learn some manners, Emma."

The sting of the slap caught the back of my thigh as well as the bottom of my butt. "Ouch!"

"Your father should've been doing this a long time ago."

The next slap was on the soft part of my bottom, and for some strange reason, it sent a flash of white-hot lightning straight into my pussy. Watching Harriet and Philip having sex had turned me on, and now my sister's brother in law was spanking me and it was…nice.

"Do you feel like a man now?"

"Oh, I'm just getting started."

I had shorts on, but my thighs were bare. He hit me again, and I gasped. "You're a pervert! I'm telling dad. He'll fire you."

"Yeah? I'll let him know about you and Harriet. Sex in the boathouse with booze and drugs."

"You fucking liar! There were no drugs."

He hit me again, but left his hand on my butt. The heat of his palms seeped through my shorts, increasing my arousal. It was so naughty being over a man's knees; a total turn on. My hair was a tangled mess around me, and my thighs stung. When he slapped me again, I moaned. A rush of sexual energy sent my heart racing.

"I think you like this, Mr. Knightley."

"This was long overdue."

I thrashed, freeing myself, but instead of fleeing, I sat on him. To be precise, I straddled one thigh, which I began to grind my pussy on. I should have been mortified by my actions, and ashamed of myself, but an uncontrollable sensation of lust overcame all of those emotions. My hands were on his shoulders, and I could barely look at him as I thrust back and forth, pushing my clit into his leg.

"Oh! Oh, my God!"

I wrapped my arms around his neck and hugged him, while pleasuring myself on his thigh. His arms enclosed my back, and he held me, letting me climb the mountain of bliss.

"Emma."

"Shut up! Ooohhh…"

Never in my life had I been this out of control. I could think of the ramifications of my actions later, but right now I was hurtling towards the most intense orgasm I could ever remember. The irony was that I was fully clothed and this was a family friend, not a lover.

"Mr…George…ooohhh…"

His hands went to my bottom, and he guided me back and forth. Being this close to him, inhaling the way his skin smelled and the hint of soap he used, left me reeling. There was something innately appealing about him that I hadn't noticed before. He had developed a rather prominent erection, having me rutting on his leg like some oversexed maniac.

"I…can't stop…ooohhhh."

The blast of release forced my head back, as I

gasped and convulsed, finally finding the release I needed. Stars exploded behind my eyelids, and I thought I heard angels singing in heaven. Collapsing on him, I breathed into his neck, trying to gather myself together.

He held me, stroking my back. "Emma."

"Shush. Don't say anything. I'm blaming it all on you. You started it. You spanked me."

He chuckled, "That was incredible."

His cock was hard beneath his shorts. There was no way I would be reciprocating. Not after getting spanked. I slid from his lap and walked away.

"Emma?"

"Good night, George." I raced to my cabin, feeling the heat of shame on my cheeks.

The PA system woke me the next morning, and I was forced to listen to, "Good morning happy campers. It's your first day at Camp Highbury. Rise and shine. Breakfast is at 0700 hours. Don't be late."

I groaned, "Thanks, dad."

Harriet giggled under her covers. "It's going to be like that every morning, isn't it?"

"Yes." After I had dressed, I turned to her. "About last night."

"Oh, shit. I lost my mind last night. I…you must think the worst of me." She shook her head. "And, Mr. Knightley. Oh, my God! How embarrassing. Are we in trouble?"

"It's none of his business what grown ups do. He was just being nosy as usual."

"You disappeared for a while. Where were you?"

I fluffed up my pillow. "Oh, I took a walk to cool off. I hate to be lectured."

"You don't think I'm a slut?"

Well, actually, yes, but… "Um, no. We were drinking

and...weird things happen when people drink."

"I really like Mr. Elton. I hope we can spend time with him today."

I glanced at my wristwatch. "Let's get to breakfast before all the bacon is gone."

"You're the best, most understanding friend ever."

Now, that was more like it. Finally, some well earned praise. As we passed the male showers, a naughty idea formed in my mind.

"We should go in and see who's in there."

Harriet's mouth fell open. "Oh, that would be so bad."

"It's good to be bad."

She giggled, "It sure is."

We tiptoed into the bathroom facility and peeked around the corner. I got a shock. It was George! He stood under the streams of water with his eyes closed. The surprise was his erection. It thrust out before him, hard and unyielding. I glanced at Harriet. Her eyes were huge. Grabbing her, we ran outside laughing.

"Oh, my God! He looks really nice naked," she said.

The tiniest prick of jealousy hit me. "He does."

"He must work out a lot. He's got muscles everywhere."

I hadn't noticed that about Mr. Knightley before, but she was right. He certainly was a fine specimen. "For sure."

"And that cock. Who do you think he was thinking about?"

I nearly choked on my own saliva. "Um, don't know."

Chapter Four

The art room was packed with noisy teens, working happily on recreating a still life of various inanimate objects. I had to teach three classes this morning and three more in the afternoon. Harriet was next door in woodworking. I'd gotten my degree in French literature with a minor in art, and, once the summer was over, I would have to find a job. I was toying with the idea of teaching, because I loved being around young people. Mr. Knightley was a professor of physics, and he enjoyed teaching. The possibility also existed of continuing my education and getting my masters.

"Miss Woodhouse. Come see this."

I went over to Stephanie and eyed her work. She'd painted a glass jar and a bundle of grapes. It looked amazingly lifelike. "That's really good." I was impressed.

"Thanks."

I wandered around the room observing the interpretations of the day's exercise. Some had chosen to do abstract versions of their inanimate objects, which wasn't exactly correct, but I wouldn't scold them for their creativity. Painting wasn't for everyone, and only a few were truly proficient at it.

"Hi." Mr. Elton had entered the room. "So this is where you hang out."

I went over to him. "Shouldn't you be working?"

"We had a hell of a time with the canoes this morning. Two overturned. It was like a bad episode of *Baywatch*."

I shook my head. "Maybe they'll have it figured out by the end of the week."

He grinned. "We can only hope."

"Harriet's next door. You should stop by and say

hello."

"I will. We gotta meet up for lunch."

"That's a great idea."

"Awesome. See you at the beach. I have a surprise."

"Oh, really?"

"Yeah."

When the morning classes were over, I went to Harriet's room. She was sweeping sawdust into a pile on the floor. Her room smelled of freshly cut wood, and a coating of dust had settled everywhere.

"It's lunch. Come on."

She glanced at me. "Where are we going?"

"To the beach. Philip has a surprise for us."

"Oohh...that could be fun."

"Hurry up with that. You should've made the kids sweep."

"We ran out of time, and they had to go."

She left the broom against a table. "I'll get this later."

As we left the building, the humidity hit us. The heat of midday created a sweltering blanket of moisture. Following the path, we made our way to the lake's edge, where Mr. Elton waited with his hands on his hips. I noticed George in the distance, and he looked unhappy. I tingled when I thought of him and what I had done to his leg last night. How embarrassing!

"We're taking a ride, ladies," said Mr. Elton.

"Oh, how fun!" Harriet flung her leg over and got in the canoe.

"Is it safe?"

"Of course. Put your life jacket on."

"Do we have to?" Harriet held an orange life preserver. "It's so bulky."

"Sorry. It's the rules."

I climbed in, and the boat began to pitch from side to side. "Shit!"

"You'll be okay. Sit quickly."

Philip shoved the canoe into the deeper water, and off we went. I glanced behind me to observe George standing by the recreation center. He watched us depart. Being Camp Supervisor, it was his job to make sure the employees were on task; however, that did not apply to our lunch hour. I felt perfectly justified taking a little canoe trip on *my* time, and, if he didn't like it, he could piss up a rope.

Ten minutes later, we reached a secluded beach, and, when we approached the shore, the bottom of the canoe ground into the sand.

Hopping out, Philip grabbed a tote bag and a blanket. "Let's have lunch."

We followed him into the woods, where he led us to a stream that gurgled over shiny rocks. A small waterfall added to the beauty of the wooded enclave, and privacy abounded. There weren't any noisy kids in the vicinity.

"Nice," I said.

"I found it yesterday." He laid out the blanket.

Harriet sat cross-legged. "What's in the bag?"

He retrieved a bottle of wine and plastic glasses. "Refreshments."

Drinking booze right before class was not a great idea. "What else?"

"Crackers and cheese."

I glanced at Harriet. "At least that's something."

"Oh, I don't care. I'll have some wine."

We ate and drank, enjoying the peaceful surrounds. I noticed the way Philip stared at Harriet, and I prided myself in the fact that I was responsible for bringing them together.

"Last night was fun," he said.

Harriet giggled, "It was."

"I wouldn't mind a lunch time quickie." Naughty insinuation laced his voice.

"Oh, what a dirty suggestion," murmured Harriet. From the look on her face, the eager expectancy, the idea appealed to her.

The bulge in Philip's pants was significant. "I won't tell, if you don't tell."

I had a sip of wine, the fluid heating my throat. It was erotic watching them have sex last night. I'd been turned on to an incredible degree.

Harriet crawled over to him. "You should let your cock out. It needs some air."

"It sure does." He unbuttoned his shorts, and his thick, pale penis thrust out. "You ladies should suck this."

"Emma, help me. Let's eat him together."

I tingled just thinking about it. "Um...I shouldn't."

"Don't be stupid. It could be fun."

What harm could come from sucking a guy's cock? We were in the middle of nowhere. Privacy surrounded us, and it was yummy looking.

"Okay."

"Oh, God, yes. You're such bad girls."

Harriet's lips were around his head, sucking vigorously. "Oh, it's so good. You should try it."

"Is this the calorie free lunch?"

She laughed, "Absolutely. But eventually, it'll be filling."

Philip groaned, "Yeah."

He smelled musky, yet delicious. I took his head in my mouth, while Harriet ran her tongue down his shaft. He moaned as a result. I hadn't had cock in quite some time, and this one was almost as nice looking as George's. Would I ever taste him, I wondered? The thought of sucking Mr.

Knightley's penis gave me an intense, pussy throbbing thrill. I lowered on him until I met up with his hairy mound.

"Aaahh…ladies…"

Harriet grabbed the wet shaft and began to deep throat him, gagging loudly. I massaged his balls and pulled on them.

"It's so good. Don't stop."

Harriet and I shared the cock, licking and sucking alternately, with aggressive determination. We must have been extraordinarily good because it wasn't long before Philip gasped, and a spurt of cream ejected, hitting Harriet's face and mouth. She held out her tongue to catch several more while I watched.

"Ooohh…yeah…nice…"

Harriet sucked him clean, licking away every last drop of spunk. I burned with arousal, but I had no idea how I would achieve release. Philip moaned, while his cock was being cleaned, looking more relaxed than I'd ever seen him.

Turning to me, he said, "Drop your pants, Emma."

I gasped. "No."

"Show us your pussy."

"Yes, I wanna see it," agreed Harriet.

I shook my head, shyness holding me hostage. "Let's get back."

A strange gleam shone in Philip's eye. "Not yet. We're just getting started."

Chapter Five

He grabbed me. "Mr. Elton!" I was thrown to the blanket, and his hand was in my shorts. "Oh! Stop it!"

"You're so wet, Emma. Lemme finger fuck you."

"Oh, good idea," chirped Harriet.

The feel of a long, hard finger over my clit had me gasping. "No." That sounded weak.

"Yes," said Philip. "You want this. It feels so good, doesn't it?"

"I…dunno." That sounded lame.

He pushed into my wetness, filling me with a long, hard finger. He kissed me and thrust his tongue into my mouth. Harriet's hands slid up my shirt and stroked my breasts. Being attacked like this certainly had its advantages. As I submitted to their eager molestation, I felt myself inching closer to bliss, which I welcomed wholeheartedly.

"Oh!"

Harriet had my shirt up, and she had undone my bra. My boobs weren't especially large, but my small B-cups were in her hands, being massaged and the nipples suckled. This shot sensation straight to my tummy and beyond, where Philip worked his wet finger in and out of my hole.

"Geor—Philip, ooohhh…." I had lost my mind. All I could think about was the finger in my pussy, pushing, prodding, and bringing about a fierce tingling; I shuddered with pleasure.

"She's getting close," he said.

"She sure is."

"Keep sucking those boobies."

Harriet giggled, "I will."

It was too much. I could feel it coming, and it was going to be good. Tossing my head back, I moaned just as the first wave hit me, sending my pulses racing and my heart pounding.

"Yeah. Cum on my finger."

I shuddered and mumbled incoherently, "Oh-God-oh-don't-keep-shit..." Philip's finger continued to move in and out, while I trembled with tiny aftershocks.

"What about me?"

We glanced at Harriet, who looked eager. She lifted her shirt over her head and undid her bra. Large, heavy looking breasts jiggled, with huge areolas around pink nipples.

"What did you have in mind?" asked Philip. He eyed her chest.

"I...could sit on your face."

"Jesus Christ! That's so dirty." He grinned. "The things I do for women."

She shoved her shorts down her legs, revealing thick thighs. I sat back mildly horrified. I had no idea what she planned to do, but I didn't want to be anywhere near when it happened.

"You're a dirty whore, Harriet."

"I am." She rubbed her breasts, bringing the massive mounds upwards. Then she let them drop, and they hung low, with hard pink nipples on each tip.

Philip laid back. "Cum get it, honey. Sit on my face."

She straddled him and lowered. "I love this. You better eat me good."

An abundance of cellulite dimpled the backs of her thighs. Philip didn't seem to mind one bit that her snatch rubbed against his mouth and her clit smashed into his nose.

"Oh, yes! You dirty boy! Fuck my hole."

The breeze brought the smell of her pussy my way,

and I cringed. She hadn't showered today, and it was noticeable. She probably smelled of sex from the night before as well. Whatever arousal I had felt earlier morphed into disgust. The sooner she had her orgasm, the better.

"Oh! Philip! It's so good. Ooohhh…"

Her hips thrust back and forth, while her tits jiggled like giant pouches of Jell-O. Mr. Elton didn't seem to mind being used like this, as his face glistened with her juices.

"Oh, God, yes! Yes! Yes! Yes!" she screamed into the forest, scaring several birds out of a nearby tree.

"What a dirty whore."

"Ooohh…I am. That was so nice." She lifted herself from his face, which glistened with wetness. "You were good."

"I try." He wiped himself on the blanket.

Totally grossed out, I wondered if he'd go around all day smelling like tuna? I hoped he washed his face after we got back. We packed up shortly thereafter and headed for the canoe. George was waiting for us as we reached the edge of the lake. He looked upset, and, glancing at my watch, I realized why. We were ten minutes late. I would have kids waiting for me in my classroom. Shit!

"Emma."

"I know, I know. I'm sorry." I took off running. He had to jog to catch up.

"We need to talk."

"Later. I have to get to class." Harriet was behind me, in a similar predicament. Our students were waiting.

"You and I will have a talk."

I couldn't look at him. "Fine."

Avoiding George was my strategy for the rest of the day, which I accomplished with great success. When I glimpsed him at the Bear Lodge talking to Jane, I made a detour and walked around the building. I was in the administration office in the late afternoon, and, after seeing him with daddy, I ducked out as fast as I could. At one point, we approached one another on a path, and I took a short cut through the dense forest to avoid him. As a consequence, I stepped into a muddy bog, and my new sneakers were utterly ruined. Ugh.

Before dinner, Harriet and I were in the boathouse, greeting a new arrival. His motorboat had just come in. He stepped onto the platform, and I felt a ping of interest. This blonde, blue-eyed hunk stood at least six feet tall and trim, with bulging muscles in all the best places. Harriet and I ogled him, as he dropped a rather large duffle bag on the floor.

"I like this place already," he declared. "Frank Churchill, at your service."

Harriet and I spoke at the same time, which was embarrassing. Now here was somebody I could get excited about. Philip was perfect for Harriet, and this gorgeous guy would be ideal for me. With matching blonde hair, we could almost be twins.

My friend gushed, "Oh, it's so good to have new arrivals. Are you a lifeguard?"

He grinned, flashing straight, white teeth. "Nope. Waterskiing. I'd be happy to give you ladies a free lesson anytime you want."

Harriet in her clumsy excitement, mis-stepped, and, a second later, she fell head first into the boat bay, which stunned everyone including the motorboat operator.

She came to the surface, sputtering, "Oh, help!"

Frank, without a moment's hesitation, jumped in fully clothed and grabbed her. He hoisted her onto the wooden platform, where she fell onto her stomach coughing.

"Uh…how…embarrassing."

"Are you all right?" I moved hair out of her face.

"Wow. First day of work and I've already rescued somebody. Awesome." Mr. Churchill hauled himself out of the water and grinned. "Like I said. I'm glad to be of service."

Harriet eyed him with water streaming down her face. "Thanks. I'm such a klutz."

I helped her to her feet.

"Ugh. I have to take a shower."

I waited for her to shower, and then we went to dinner directly. We sat at a table with George, Frank, and Jane. The conversation revolved around Frank's chivalrous rescue of my friend, and every detail of his heroics were expounded upon, until I beamed at him happily, marveling that he could very well be the perfect man. Jane, doe-eyed and far too gorgeous for my liking, smiled brightly as him, as did Harriet. Poor George was all but ignored, and, when I stole a glance at him, he looked perturbed. I'd tried all day not to think about what had happened last night and this morning. It seemed the sight of his naked body was burned into my brain. When I closed my eyes, I saw him in the shower, moving the bar of soap over his wet, muscled body, and then down to his bulging cock, which—"

"Emma! Are you listening to me?" asked Harriet.

I nodded. "Sure."

"Don't you think Frank is in the wrong job? He really should be a lifeguard."

"Oh, yeah."

"He's got talents we can only dream about."

He laughed, "Aw, come on. Don't you think that's pushing it a bit?"

"Not at all," she said.

Harriet beamed with pleasure, having hijacked the dinner conversation and garnering all of the attention. Even

George smiled at her with appreciation, which irritated me. Since when had I become a wallflower?

"There's a dance tonight," I said.

"Oh, my God," uttered Harriet. "I so thought I was gonna drown, like really. I must've swallowed a gallon of lake water. You think I'll get dysentery now?"

George patted her on the back. "If you start puking, I'll get you a bucket."

"Thanks."

Feeling ignored and miserable, I slunk into my seat and glared at Harriet, as she continued to babble on about her near death experience. Later, in the recreation center, the disco ball had been enabled, and horrible music from the seventies played. I glanced at daddy and scolded him with a look. He shrugged unapologetically. He loved old people music, and we would be forced to dance to Led Zeppelin and Fleetwood Mack, not to mention other ancient bands from the days of bellbottoms and beards. Ugh.

As the music played and people danced, I discovered Jane and Frank Churchill together, while Harriet and Philip swayed to the music with their arms around each other. Anger pricked me. Frank was supposed to be mine! Disgusted, I turned and bumped into George.

His eyes shone puzzlingly. "I think we should dance, Emma."

"No."

"Yes."

Chapter Six

How Deep Is Your Love from the Bee Gees played, and as George led me out onto the crowded dance floor, I had a moment of surreal incongruity. He was the last person I wanted to spend time with, because he exasperated and confused me.

He drew me to him. "You've been avoiding me."

"No I haven't."

"Don't lie, Emma."

"I'm not."

"We can play this game all you want, but we both know what's happening here."

"What the hell are you talking about?"

"The rec center last night."

"I think Frank saving Harriet really shows his character, don't you?" I had to change the subject. "I first thought that he'd be great for her, but now I'm thinking maybe I want him for myself."

"He's not into you."

I gasped, "How the hell do you know?"

"A guy knows these things. You can tell by the way he looks at Jane. He's hot for her."

"Ugh! NO way. I don't get that at all."

"You're only seeing what you want to see."

I ignored that. "Harriet loves Phillip Elton, and he's crazy about her. There's a match made in heaven right there."

"Wrong again."

"Shut up."

"He's out to get in her pants, but nothing beyond that."

"Sometimes relationships start with sex. Then they

grow."

"Not in this case."

I harrumphed. "Oh, be quiet. What do you know anyway?" I saw daddy by the record player and waved to him. He nodded and smiled. "You're in no position to give dating advice, since you've been single for how long? You're pushing forty, right?" His grip tightened around me, and his lips were near my ear, which made me tingle with pleasure.

"You're a spoiled little brat, Emma."

The insult affected me in the most bizarre way. Instead of angering me, I began to tremble with arousal, wanting him to whisper something else low and intimate.

"I'm nowhere near forty. I haven't been single that long."

My arms snaked around his neck, and I pressed myself to him, remembering exactly how he looked without clothes on. The hardness of his erection pressed against my stomach.

"Emma." He drew me away to a dark corner and pressed me into a nook between a bookcase and the wall, where we were hidden from sight.

As his lips descended, I knew what he was going to do. "No!"

But it was too late. He kissed me, making my head bump into the wall. The feel of his tongue had me gasping with pleasure. He savaged my eager mouth with just the right amount of pressure and persistence, as his tongue fought with mine in a sensual dance.

"Oh, God, Emma."

He kissed my neck, gently biting the skin. My fingertips dug into his shoulders, while he pushed himself into me, grinding his erection against my tummy.

"Miss Woodhouse?" said a voice. "Is that you?"

I gasped in horror. One of my students stood not more than three feet way with an amused, yet interested expression on her face. I pushed at Mr. Knightley, and exclaimed, "Get your paws off me! Men. I can't believe that. What a pig." I brushed by him, leaving him yet again, with a hard, painful erection. "Hi, Sammy. What can I do for you?"

I danced with several cute lifeguards and a member of the climbing staff. Then I got into a conga line with Harriet, which was a riot. All the while, George stood with daddy, watching with an unreadable expression. Afterwards, we led the Macarena, which was lots of fun. The entire camp got involved, and we followed Harriet, who seemed to have the movements down pat.

At one point, Harriet asked Mr. Elton to dance, and he brushed her off, to my annoyance. I felt horrible for my friend in that instance, until George intervened and led her out to the dance floor, where they boogied to one of Michael Jackson's earlier hits. I felt a rush of pride for George in that moment, being the gentleman that he was. Harriet seemed to enjoy his company, beaming and flirting with him.

Later that evening, after the dance had ended, I found myself with Jane and Harriet in one of the older cabins. We had a bottle of whisky, which Jane had smuggled in. So much for a dry camp.

"I think Frank is so cute," said Jane.

I was beginning to warm up to her. "He has possibilities."

Harriet took a swig of the bottle. "All the guys here have possibilities. I can't remember having this much fun, but..." she glanced at me warily, "Emma won't like this."

"What?"

"I kinda like the cook."

"Who?" She handed me the whisky, and I took a sip, coughing. It burned all the way down my throat.

"Mr. Martin. The head cook. I talked to him earlier. He has a bucket of unopened peanut butter, if we want it."

I pushed her and laughed, "Oh, not him. He's not the one for you."

She shrugged. "Why not?"

I grimaced. "Cause he's not upwardly mobile. You have to aim higher, Harriet. You don't wanna be married to a loser."

Her features twisted unpleasantly. "He's not a loser. He's working to save money for automotive school. He wants to fix BMW's. Is that hoity-toity enough for you?"

Oh, shit. I'd pissed her off. "Look, I didn't mean it like that."

She got to her feet. "Sure you didn't. Not everyone can be a doctor's daughter, Emma." She stormed off in a huff.

I glanced at Jane. "Oh, shit."

Jane shrugged. "Have a drink. She'll get over it."

On my way to the cabin, I loitered, not wanting to face Harriet. I hadn't gone far when a man approached. In the moonlight he looked tall and menacing, but, on closer inspection, it was none other than George. I tried to go by him quickly, but he caught my arm.

"Emma."

"Let go."

"We have to talk. I've been looking for you for the last hour. Where have you been?"

"Nowhere."

"Have you been drinking?"

"Nope."

He pulled me to him. "You're lying. I can smell it on you."

"So?"

His chest rumbled with laughter. "You just can't behave, can you?"

"What's it to you? Why don't you go find the lovely Ms. Fairfax. I left her with a bottle of Jack Daniels. She should be…well marinated by now."

"Inebriated, just like you are."

"Yeah, whatever."

"Let me see you to your cabin."

I hesitated, remembering the fight with Harriet. "Uh…I can't go there. My bunkmate's pissed at me."

"Let's go to mine then."

"Uh, oh, no. That's not a good idea."

"It's the best idea yet."

As he steered me in a new direction, I should have refused. Mr. Knightley of all people was not someone I should be left alone with, especially since he was such an amazing kisser and his penis was really long and yummy looking. *Stop thinking about it!*

He shoved the door open with one foot and pushed me inside. I turned on him. "Who's lacking manners now? You practically kidnap me, and…you force me into your room."

Slamming the door, he advanced on me, fire blazing in his eyes. "You and I have some unfinished business."

I swallowed hard. He looked so good with his unkempt hair and day old beard. *It's just the booze talking, Emma. By morning, you'll be angry with him all over again.*

He grabbed me, and we fell to his bed, which was unmade and on the small side. His lips covered mine, as he drove his tongue into my mouth. I moaned. He tasted so good; I wanted to eat him up. He pulled my t-shirt over my head and struggled to unhook my bra.

"Let me." I paused to look at him. "We shouldn't

be doing this."

"I think you're wrong about that. This is exactly what we should be doing."

I shook my head. "No. It'll be awkward tomorrow. We're family."

"By marriage only. Are you gonna take that damn thing off, or do I have to do it?" he growled.

"I'll take it off." I loosened the bra, and it hung limply. "You hate me."

His head snapped in surprise. "What makes you think that?"

"You tell me all the time what a pest I am."

"Oh, Emma."

"It's true."

He held my face. "You have a lot to learn about men, honey. I don't hate you at all. Not even close."

"You don't?"

"No."

His lips descended, silencing the conversation.

Chapter Seven

I'd never been with anyone before where it felt like the other person was an extension of myself. We melded together perfectly, our bodies eager and needy, in blissful communion. He was on me, with his lips to my ear kissing and sucking an earlobe. My hands were under his shirt, caressing his back, feeling the heat of his skin.

"Oh, Emma."

"Take it off. I want you naked."

He chuckled, "Yes, ma'am."

I pushed my shorts down, panties and all, until I was entirely naked. He shoved his pants to his ankles and kicked them off. Then he covered me with his nude perfection, settling between my thighs, with his hardness pressing to me, intimately.

"Oh, my God, George."

"I'm so sorry, baby."

The next thing I knew, he'd entered me, filling my pussy with that magnificent cock. The intrusion was staggering, and I ached for a second, having not been totally prepared to receive him. If I thought he would be an attentive and gentle lover, I was wrong. He began to thrust into me almost carelessly, his breath in my neck, gasping and ragged. Within moments, he shuddered and groaned, emptying his seed. I held him for long moments, wondering what was going to happen next. Should I get dressed and leave now?

"That was...horrible," he muttered. "I'm mortified."

"Um...okay. It was okay."

"No, it wasn't. I've been fantasizing about you for so long. Just give me a minute, and I'll have a little more control."

He lay next to me with his hand on my belly. Rubbing my flat, toned skin, he began to drift to my pussy. His finger brushed over me, and then sunk into my dripping hole. I could feel his sperm on my inner thighs.

George drew near and kissed my neck. "We don't have to rush. We've got all night."

The coldness of his spunk made me slightly uncomfortable. "I need a tissue or something."

"No you don't."

He kissed my tummy, and then he descended towards my pussy, one soft kiss at a time. He wasn't going to go down there, was he? Spreading my thighs, he settled himself between and began to lick my labia, eliciting a tingling feeling there that I was not prepared for. Embarrassed and slightly grossed out, I wanted to tell him to stop, but he continued to eat me, driving his tongue into my sopping hole, extracting his jizz.

"Isn't that gross?"

"No."

I threw my head back and let him have me. If it turned him on to eat his own spunk, then so be it. It was making me horribly excited, and little flutters of pleasure danced around in my belly, making me moan and gasp. His finger drove into me, and he thrust it in and out, pleasuring and seducing.

"Oh, George."

"Get on your stomach."

"What?"

"Be a good girl, and do as I ask. Finger yourself."

I rolled over, slid my hand to my pussy, and began to touch myself. He came in behind me and plunged his hard cock deep.

"Oh!"

He had recovered quickly. As he began to ride me from behind, the gradual build of release beckoned, teasing me with the promise of mind-blowing bliss. This position had several advantages, allowing his cock to thrust deeply, hitting against a hidden erogenous zone, which added to my pleasure and brought on the orgasm that much faster.

"George!" I shuddered with little convulsions and spasms, forcing my face into the bed and moaning loudly. "Ooohh…"

"That's it, Emma. Ride it out." He stroked me with his super hard cock, until every last pulse dwindled away. Then he slid free. "Would you like this?"

"Yes."

I took him into my hands, feeling wetness on him. He smelled musky, not just from my pussy, but from his own spunk. I thought I would find this off putting and unpalatable, yet, remarkably, the opposite was true. As I sucked greedily, I was amazed that we had actually had sex. I'd known him for years since his brother was married to my older sister. It was naughty to be doing this, to be sucking his cock, and listening to his groans as I pleasured him, until I gagged. This certainly appealed to my naughty side, and I hoped this would not be a one-night only event. Now that I had sampled George's delights, I prayed I would be able to indulge often.

"Oh, my God, Emma!"

He pulled himself from my mouth just as he squirted. I held out my tongue hoping to catch it, but the spray caught my forehead, cheeks, and hair. It was out of control.

"I'm sorry," he chuckled. "My bad."

I brushed a wet strand of hair out of my face. "Are you always like this?"

He collapsed on the bed. "No. I only embarrass

myself with you." He pulled me to him. "Come here."

I snuggled into his warm chest. "I have to go."

"Just be with me for a while, then you can go."

I yawned. "Okay."

I ended up staying the night. The next morning, I embarked on the walk of shame back to my cabin. It was early, even before daddy's PA announcement had gone off. George and I passed the men's bathroom, and I noticed the cleaning cart out front.

I blurted, "Ugh. What a horrible job to have to clean the shitter. Why anyone would want to do it is beyond me." As we passed, I realized, to my mortification, that Ms. Bates had been standing in the entrance, mopping. She had heard every word.

George glared at me, and I found myself, yet again, at the receiving end of one of his looks of disapproval. I walked on with my head down.

"Emma! She heard that. She heard every word."

I refused to look at him.

He grabbed my arm. "You're going to have to apologize for that. Not everyone in life has it as easy as you do. Not everyone has the advantages you have."

I felt horrible. I began to cry. "I'm going to my cabin."

He drew me to him. "Emma."

"I'm not a bad person." I sniffed into his shirt.

"I know you're not. You mean well by trying to find dates for your friends, and you're a great teacher. I've listened to you when you didn't know I was there. You're fantastic with them, honey, but you lack an understanding about people. Ms. Bates works because she needs the money and she's not qualified for a better job. She's stuck in her life. Have some compassion, for Christ's sake."

"You hate me."

"I don't hate you."

"You like Jane better."

This flabbergasted him. Surprise lit his eyes. "Did I spend last night with Jane? I spent it with you, you silly girl."

I sniffed. "I'm not a girl." I pushed at him. "I have to shower. Then I have to find Ms. Bates and apologize."

He watched me walk away.

What became the longest, most humbling day of my life began shortly after my shower. Before class, I found Ms. Bates, and I apologized. She told me about her circumstances, her health issues, her sister's death, her son's drug addiction, and then I felt even worse. Harriet was still mad at me, and she ignored me at lunch and ate with Jane and Frank, while I picked at my carrots with the prongs of my fork. When class was over, I wandered up the path to the Administration building to find daddy. He was in his office.

"Daddy?"

"Yes, dear?"

"Do you think I'm a bad person?"

This question surprised him. "Of course not, Emma. Why would you say that?"

"I'm…just…I don't know."

He stood and came over. "Has something happened?"

"George thinks I'm a brat."

He chuckled, "Don't pay any attention to that. He's only teasing you, honey."

"Do you like him?"

"Of course I like George. He's an outstanding person."

"Am I an outstanding person?"

He hugged me. "You tell George to stop picking on

you. Don't let him make you feel bad. He's really very fond of you, Emma."

Daddy smelled of minty *Bengay*. "Is your shoulder bothering you still?"

"A little. That'll teach me to move furniture by myself." He stepped away from me. "Now, no more moping. You're a fine young woman, Emma. You went to a first class college. You work well with kids, and you've held the family together after your mother passed away. You're my shining star, and don't you forget it."

"I say mean things without thinking."

"We all do that. No one is perfect."

He did have a point, and I had apologized to Ms. Bates. The lingering feelings of self-loathing followed me well into the night, when the camp was inundated with rain. I sat in my cabin alone, wondering where Harriet was and listening to the crack of thunder overhead. When the lights flickered and the electricity went off, I threw on a raincoat and headed for the Bear Lodge.

Chapter Eight

The lodge's fireplace roared with a toasty blaze. The building was lit with gas lamps and candlelight and filled with teens escaping their darkened cabins. Some held video games, while others played cards to pass the time. The storm raged outside, rain splashing against the windowpanes. Frank and Jane came in laughing and wet, and I was instantly jealous.

Harriet approached. "I wondered where you were."

"I want to apologize for last night. I'm sorry I'm such a stuck up bitch."

Her look softened. "It's okay. I really like Robert, but someone else has caught my fancy." She winked. "Ever since that morning we saw Mr. Knightley in the shower, that's all I've been able to think about. He sure is one hot hunk of—"

I shook my head vigorously. "No! He's so not right for you."

Her hands went to her hips. "Really?"

"I mean, I...he's old. He's nearly forty. Wouldn't you want someone younger?"

"You don't seem to approve of anyone I date, Emma, and I'm beginning to get really pissed off. George isn't good enough for me, is that what you're saying?"

I whispered, "I kinda like him."

"I bet you do."

"I was with him last night."

Her mouth dropped open. "That's where you were. I wondered whose cabin you were in."

I glanced around to make sure no one was listening. "He's wonderful, Harriet. I'm sorry, but we...we are...I think we're together now." Or were we?

I thought she would blow her top. She looked angry, yet hopeful. "I'm going to find Robert."

"You are?"

"I shoulda listened to my instincts in the first place."

"Really?"

"I don't care if you disapprove of him, Ms. Woodhouse. He's my kind of guy. I like 'em rough around the edges. I don't want anyone smarter than I am. Philip was way outta my league, and we both know it. Frank's hot for Jane. You have George. I'm going after the cook."

I hugged her. "I've done it again! Another match made in heaven."

She stepped out of the embrace. "Uh, girlfriend, oh, no. You had nothin' to do with this, so don't think you're taking the credit."

I smiled sheepishly. "Never mind. You did it all on your own."

"You bet your ass I did."

George was across the room, smiling. He was looking at me, wasn't he? I glanced behind me to make sure it wasn't Jane he was so friendly with. As Harriet departed, he came over. Taking my hand, he pulled me to another part of the lodge.

"Where are we going?" I was suddenly in his arms being kissed passionately. "Oh, I like this."

He held me close. "I love you, Emma. I've loved you for a long time."

I gasped, "You're kidding?"

He shook his head. "We're perfect for each other. I've been waiting so long to get this off my chest."

"You have?"

He nodded. "You're finally done with school. There's no reason why you can't move in with me. I want you in my life, Ms. Woodhouse."

"Oh, George." I hugged him. A rush of tenderness brought tears to my eyes. "I love you too."

"Will you marry me, Emma?"

"But isn't that weird?"

"How do you mean?"

"My sister's married to your brother, and now I'll be married to my sister's husband's brother. I'm so confused."

He kissed my hand. "There's nothing weird about that. Let's find your father and make it official."

I grinned. "Okey-dokey. Lead the way."

The End

Made in the USA
Middletown, DE
18 June 2025